The Forest

of

Fallen Stars

Elfie Riverdell

First published independently in Great Britain in 2019
Edition 2 - published 2021

Elfie Riverdell
Independently published

For Jake

Chapter One

Nobody knows when the ceremonies began.
For centuries, people have told of them. Stories
of children dressed in white, lined up at the
edge of the forest. Tales of parents planting
kisses on foreheads and sending their beloved
children into the forest, praying to the gods for
their safe return. I looked up at the Forest
Father, his golden robes swaying gently in the
breeze. His face was worn, but soft and
welcoming. He didn't seem to notice the fear in
our eyes as one by one he sent us off into the
darkness. I was one of the oldest in the village,
so I was near the front of the line. Four

children had entered the forest and returned by the time I took my place beside the Forest Father. I thought back to the year before, when my sister Maure had been of age. A shiver ran down my spine at the memory of my mother's tears, as she stood at the edge of the river, waiting. It had been almost two hours before Maure appeared at the edge of the forest, limping, her eyes cast down at the ground. The Forest Father placed a chain of flowers around my neck, and ushered me closer to the trees. His hands were pale but damp with sweat, and his eyes hid the uncertainty in his heart."Don't be afraid child." He patted my shoulder, giving me a warm smile. It did not comfort me. I stepped into the trees, my bare feet feeling their way through the darkness. I could hear voices, both human and animal surrounding me. I wondered how many of the voices belonged to my friends. I took one last glance at the Forest Father, his white hair blowing softly in the wind as he watched me from the edge of the woods. Turning back, I stared into the darkness in front of me, trees crowded together so close that I could barely see a path through them. Maure had told me that it only took around a hundred steps to reach the clearing, but her legs were long and elegant, unlike my own. It may take me a few steps more.Taking in deep breaths, I focused on the smell of the damp moss to calm my nerves. I counted my steps. Twenty four, twenty five.Someone ran past me, but I couldn't see their face. A fog was beginning to envelop me, dragging me deeper into the woods. I stood on a bramble, and a sharp pain shot up my leg. My feet burned with the sting of the nettles, and I bit down hard on my lip.

 Forty seven, forty eight.

 Another voice, more bare feet breaking twigs beside me. I looked around frantically, desperate to see a familiar face.

The voices seemed content though, and I let myself take comfort in that. I didn't want to hear the screams, the terror.

I only wanted to hear the sound of gentle steps away from the forest. The sounds of happy, relieved children returning to their families.

Seventy two, Seventy three.

I saw it, ahead in the distance. Maure was right, another twenty or so steps and I'd be there. It would be my turn. I stumbled over fallen branches, throwing my arms around in an attempt to regain my balance. The fog cleared.

Ninety nine, one hundred.

I had found it.

...

In the middle of the clearing sat a small golden candle, its flame swaying softly in the night breeze.

I took another deep breath, wiped the sweat from my hands on my tunic and sat beside the candle. I tried to remember the steps of the ritual, searching my mind for what the Forest Father had taught us. I cast myself back to the days I'd spent huddled with the other children in the centre of the village, listening anxiously to what the Forest Father had to say. We had spent months learning the ritual, practicing and building up our strength. We would fight together for hours, with blunt weapons and heavy cloth bags tied to our backs.

Some children were gifted companions that could not protect them, small creatures like snakes. We had to be prepared.

"O Goddess of light, take this offering and grant me my companion." I whispered, slipping the flowers from my neck and placing them on a slowly growing pile beside me.

 I dropped my hands to my lap and waited. The evening wind blew my hair from my face, sending the curls cascading down my back like an onyx river.

Time seemed to go still, and I had no notion of how long I had been sitting in the candle light before a rustling ahead caught my attention.

I stood up, bracing myself for what was about to happen.

"O creature of warmth, come to me and protect me from the God of Darkness"

I fell to my knees, my eyes closed and palms outstretched. The smell of the burning wax beside me filled my lungs, and I breathed it in. This was the moment my entire life had been leading up to.

Long moments passed before something wet touched my hand, and I opened my eyes to see that it was in fact a nose.

The nose of a large black dog, with bright green eyes and a coat as soft and dark as that of a raven. I placed my hand on its head and whispered my gratitude to the goddess, before standing to my full height - not that much taller than the dog.

It stared up at me, its eyes the same colour as the trees surrounding us. I'd never seen a dog like this as a companion. In fact, I'd never seen anyone with a dog at all. Wolves, foxes and small bears were common.

Snakes, rats, owls and deer were also given by the Goddess quite regularly. But dogs were not common here.

Some villages not far from ours breed wolves and keep them as pets. Others keep dogs to guard land, but here we have only wild dogs, no domesticated animals at all. Our ancestors saw it as disrespectful to the Goddess.

 "Come." I said, making my way to the edge of the clearing. The dog followed silently, it's huge paws padding softly over the dusty ground. Leaves rustled around us, and I looked warily over my shoulder.

 Now the danger began.

Chapter Two

It wasn't long before we found ourselves
surrounded. This part of the ceremony was
your companion's chance to fight for your life.
They must protect you from the wild. Everyone
knew what would happen, we'd heard the tales
and we'd seen it with our own eyes. Every year
children would stumble through the forest, and
return traumatised, with shredded tunics, open
wounds and terrified faces.

 The wild creatures always attacked, whether
through fear or through anger. Either way, they
would do a lot of damage if your companion
didn't protect you. Companions are wild at
heart after all, and their soul never changes.

It is through fighting against danger that they take on their roles as a protector. They learn your strengths and weaknesses, and fight alongside you the way they do with their own kind.

The forest had grown dark, and I was navigating more by touch than sight.

I could feel the earth beneath my feet warming, and I knew I was heading out of the forest, back towards the village.

The wind blew the branches above and the moon peaked between the leaves, casting flecks of light onto the forest floor. A rumble came from across the path, and I looked up to see a bear watching us.

I stood instinctively behind my companion, hoping that if we stayed still, the wild creatures would move on, and leave without attacking us. Behind the bear's towering form, stood a wolf and a huge wild dog. Both were bigger than my companion, but he stood fiercely beside me, his head high and his growl echoing around us.

The bear flew towards me and I gasped, squeezing my eyes shut. A branch snapped under the animal's weight and I threw my hands in front of me, crouching lower to the ground. My breath burst from my lungs in huge gasps, but I forced them to slow and waited for my heart to stop racing.

Lights danced across my eyelids, and I wondered if the moon was peeking through the trees, curious to see what was happening down in our own world.

When I opened my eyes, the bear was retreating, it's opal eyes full of fear.

A dark line ran down its spine where the hair stood on end, and the wolf growled at us as we backed away slowly.

My companion lunged forward, snapping at the animals. They had stopped circling us, and were seemingly frozen where they stood. I didn't have time to think. They were backing away, the wild dog's tail between its legs. I put a shaking hand on my dog's back, my breathing ragged.

"Come now!" I said sharply, backing away from the wild creatures as they dropped their heads and watched us leave.

There was no time to consider what had just happened, I just ran. The journey back from the clearing is supposed to be horrific. It's supposed to be terrifying and traumatic. That's what bonds you with your companion.

I ran through the forest, my heart pounding in my ears. I just had to get out of there, out of the darkness.

My companion raced alongside me, his eyes focused on every step I made.

I remembered the children of past ceremonies, lining up outside the healer's house. Broken bones were not uncommon, and neither were near-fatal wounds.

The companions usually took more injuries than the children, but it was very rare for a child to return unscathed.

I thought back to last year's ceremony, and how one of the young girls had looked as she crawled from the edge of the forest. She'd lost a hand, and had never quite recovered from the shock. I'd never seen an injury like it, never heard of anything so awful.

Her name was Sil, and she was much smaller than Maure.

Not much taller than me in fact, and much weaker. We all worried about her as she entered the forest almost three hours before, and the sight of her returning sent a ripple of panic through the village.

The healer's apprentice had rushed forward, cradling Sil in his arms as he carried her through the crowd.

 I burst out of the forest, trying to ignore the searing pain in my side from the stitch that had developed as I ran. I caught a glimpse of my mother, tears streaming down her face as she pushed through the crowd. I wondered how long I'd been gone.

 She threw her arms around me, embracing me as if it were the last time she would ever have the chance. My father ushered my siblings towards me, a grim expression on his face. He was a large man, not in size, but in the way he carried himself.

His hair was cropped short against his head, and he was one of the few men in the village that was clean-shaven. His eyes were such a dark brown that they were almost black. It was hard to distinguish between the iris and the pupil.

He looked me over, crouching to my height, checking for any injuries.

His eyes searched me head to toe before he nodded reassuringly at my mother. He placed a hand on my head and stood up. My younger sister Lila grabbed at my legs, hugging them to her tiny body and grinning up at me.

"You got puppy!" She said, as if I hadn't noticed.

My mother had dressed her in a green dress, a light wool with a white trim. There was dirt up one side where she'd curled up on the grass and fallen asleep waiting for me. One of her ponytails was higher than the other, and I smiled down at her as I fixed her hair.

I looked around at the other families from the village. Mothers were embracing children, friends celebrating.

The noise was overwhelming. Maure stepped forward last, her eyes focused on the dog sitting beside me. She crouched down, her dark, wavy hair falling into her face as she stared into its eyes.

"What will you call it?" She asked, looking up at me for a split second before returning her attention to the smudge of black fur.

"Skygge." I whispered, stroking his ears. "I call him shadow."

Chapter Three

The ceremony continued for almost six hours
after I was reunited with my family. There were
many children to perform the ritual this year,
and by the time it had ended we were all
crawling to our beds. Lila had fallen asleep
again not long after I had returned, and I
carried her to her cot in my arms. Maure and I
were both very protective over her, and in some
ways we treated her like our own.
I spent many hours reading to her, dancing
with her and telling her stories of magic and
long-lost princesses.

My mother stood behind me as I rocked the cot a little, sitting down to admire the innocence my sister still possessed. Sometimes I wondered what she would go through later on. I thought a lot about what her companion might be, and I liked to imagine that it would be an owl. She was such a wise and inquisitive child, it seemed only fitting that her companion would be too. I watched a smile play on her lips, her face warm and pink.

Her cheeks were full, round and healthy. She was small for her age, but strong.

"I can't imagine seeing the day when Lila will have to go through all this." I sighed, turning to my mother. She was a beautiful woman, dark skin and warm features.

Her hair was much longer than mine and it fell past her hips in soft curls. She sat elegantly, her hands resting in her lap.

Her companion, a small red fox, lay by the door, watching us curiously. I wondered if my father's wolf was watching him chop the firewood.

"You were brave today." She told me, taking my hand.

"No braver than the rest." I shrugged, giving a weak smile. My mother dropped my hand and sat on the edge of her bed. She was playing nervously with the sheet, avoiding my eyes.

"I know they didn't attack you." She said finally. The way she spoke made me feel as if I'd done something wrong. I felt myself go suddenly still, as if I should have been hiding some great secret. We all grew up hearing stories from the older children about the ferocious wild creatures, and their attacks during the ceremonies.

Wild creatures are untamed, untouched by the Goddess. They are the ones without human companions.

They fear us, and we fear them too. That's how it's always been. People who ventured into the woods to hunt birds and rabbits often went missing, or returned half dead.

A friend of my father had been well known for hunting rabbits in the woods, unafraid of the wild creatures that lurked in the darkness. His name was Hagan and he was a large man with legs like tree trunks.

His hair was wild and red, but dirty red rather than a bright copper. Every day he stalked into the forest with his bow and his axe, but one morning he didn't return. It was three days before he was found, bloody and within an inch of his life. The healer cured him of his infections, but the wounds never fully healed. He never walked again.

He claimed it had been a bear that attacked him, but it may have been wolves.

I looked up at my mother.

"There was a bear that tried to attack... and a wolf and a wild dog too but-" I began, but she raised a hand to stop me. I settled beside her on the bed. My hair fell into my face, sticking to my forehead. I swiped it away with my thumb.

"There will be a reason." She admitted, pushing a strand of hair from my face absently. "You just have to figure out what it is."

...

I found Maure in her bedroom, braiding her
hair and humming a sweet tune to Midnight.

We'd all been slightly shocked when Maure had
slipped out of the forest holding a black snake
around her wrist.
She'd always been frightened of snakes, and
was anxious at the idea of being gifted one.
But she was instantly attached to the tiny
creature, with its intense and unnaturally large
eyes. The onyx serpent wound its way around
my sisters leg and seemed to be falling asleep,
it's tongue tasting the air as I sat down against
the wall.
He had grown since Maure had been gifted
him, and was almost as long now as she was
tall, but still slim with dark iridescent scales
that shone in the light.

Our parents were busy doing chores around the house, and Lila stayed sound asleep in her cot in their bedroom.

I could hear the distant sound of our father chopping wood in the garden, and smell the soup my mother was cooking on the stove. It felt good to be surrounded by normal life again. Everything stops in the weeks leading up to your ceremony. A nervous energy threatens to eat you from the inside out, as family test anxiously you on what you must say and do during the ritual.

"Maure?"

"Alura?" She raised an eyebrow at me, tying off her braid with a thin strip of leather and throwing it over her shoulder. She turned to me, a mischievous smile on her golden face, as if expecting some gossip. Maure and I were not alike in many ways.

We both had our mother's dark hair, and our father's strong features, but that's where the majority of our similarities ended.

Maure was funny, giggly and easily excited. I, on the other hand was quieter, fiercer, and much more serious. I looked at my sister uneasily.

"When you were given Midnight..." I whispered, looking at her companion and hoping nobody could overhear us. "Did you get attacked?"

Maure sighed heavily, leaning back in her chair. She'd never been one to discuss her ritual too openly. She preferred to discuss happier occasions, and liked to pretend that bad things never happened.

I watched nervously as she lifted up the hem of her skirt to reveal a scar across her right thigh. It was almost three inches long, and looked as if it had come from a pretty deep cut. She flicked her eyes at me.

"I had to fight them off myself. Midnight is venomous, but he was too small to protect me."

I wasn't sure if her answer made me feel better or worse.

Suddenly it seemed to hit her what an unusual question it was, for being attacked during your ritual was pretty standard.

She turned back to me so quickly that her braid smacked me in the face.

"Didn't you?"

I fumbled with the hem of my own dress.

"Well, yes I did." I nodded. "But only one of the creatures came towards me. They must have been frightened of Skygge I suppose." I admitted, looking down, feeling almost embarrassed.

The concerned look on Maure's face was soon pushed aside for a more excited one.

"Of course they were!" She beamed, stroking Skygge as he strolled towards her. "Look at him, I'd be scared too!"

I knew she was only trying to make me feel better, make me feel as if it was normal, but I knew it wasn't.

I'd been preparing for years, we all had. As soon as we were old enough, we'd practice fighting against each other, building up our strength.

Nobody could avoid the ceremonies, so we each tried to become the strongest in our class. The stronger you are, the more chance you have of getting out of the forest without life threatening wounds. The fiercer you are, the more chance you have of fighting the wild creatures off.

Midnight was tasting the air around Skygge as he lay against the wall between Maure and I. He slithered across the wooden floor, curled up against Skygge's thick fur, and closed his beady eyes.

"He's trusting." I nodded to Maure, and she smiled.

"Because I trust you."

Chapter Four

It had been raining for days, almost a week
straight since the ceremony. The smell of wet
dog followed me everywhere, but I was
beginning to like it. It was comforting. I liked
knowing I was not alone, that I had someone
keeping me safe at all times. At night when the
memory of the ceremony ran through my
mind, I listened to Skygge breathing beside me,
his head propped up on my bed. He brought
me great comfort, and followed me everywhere
I went.

He sat with me when I ate, and slept with me
during the night. At dinner he would curl up

beside my mother's companion; a small red
fox.

In the morning he would chase my father's wolf
through the house, yapping and jumping up at
him playfully. The sound of his heavy paws
against the ground was relaxing, and I felt safer
having him around.

 I trudged my way up the hill towards the
Forest Father's house. It was a small building,
surrounded by pine trees.

He liked to live alone, away from the centre of
the village. He was an elderly man, he liked
peace and quiet. As I reached his door, I called
out to him. Hearing no reply I knocked softly
and waited for him to answer. A few moments
later he appeared, a thick wool tunic keeping
him warm in the cold autumn air.

He came forward, peering around the outside
of his house before his eyes met mine.

 "Alura my child! Come in, come in!" He
ushered me into the house, wrapping a blanket
around my shoulders.

Skygge settled himself in front of the fire, and promptly fell asleep. I watched his chest rise and fall with his gentle breathing, but I could tell that he was still aware of his surroundings.

"What brings you here in this weather Alura?" The Forest Father's eyes were a cool green, not far off the shade of the pine trees that protected his home from the winter winds. Most people in our village had mossy green eyes, it was a trait almost all of us possessed. He set a small copper kettle on the fire, rubbing his pale hands together to warm them.

"I want to ask a question about the ceremony." I told him, trying to sound confident, as if I wasn't shaking in my boots. He frowned at me.

"Were you hurt?" He asked, looking me up and down for injuries. "I can ask the healer to check on you."

"No Father, I was not injured. That is why I am here."

He seemed to change then, looking at me more sceptically. He looked over at Skygge, whose ears were twitching subtly as he listened even during his sleep.

"A bear began to attack, but did not come close. The wild creatures seemed terrified to attack me." I explained.

"This is certainly unusual child, but I would not worry yourself about it.

Perhaps it is his colour." the Forest Father suggested, tapping his chin and nodding at Skygge. "Black is an uncommon colour for wild dogs in these parts. Perhaps that is what threw them."

His lip twitched nervously as he spoke, and I eyed him suspiciously.

I had been brought up to be trusting of my elders, but I could always tell when someone was hiding something.

I'd heard of many people with black wolves as companions, and several villages on the west side of the island kept black dogs as pets. I didn't understand why black would be such an uncommon colour for a wild dog, many other animals had similar colourings.

—

"Maybe." I nodded, although I wasn't sure.
The Forest Father looked at me as if he was deciding whether or not to tell me the truth. He frowned, looking from me to Skygge.

"Have you ever heard of a wild creature not attacking a child and their companion?" I didn't like the idea of having the something kept from me.

"No child, I can't say that I have." He shook his head, sighing heavily. I looked over at the fire but Skygge was no longer there. Panic seeped into my bones and I stood up, searching around me frantically.

"Skygge!" I screamed, but a hand closed over my mouth and I was still.

"Don't make a sound." Came the Forest Father's whisper. I swallowed hard, and lifted my hand to tell him I understood.
He released me, stepping away and rubbing his temples. "Where is he?" I demanded, frightened and angry.

"He is doing his duty. He is protecting you." the Forest Father said, rubbing his temples. I heard barking coming from outside of the house, and dashed towards the door before the the Forest Father could stop me.

He was calling my name as he tried to keep up with me, hobbling down the hall as I ran past the kitchen. I was seconds away from falling through the open door, into the rain and wind, when hands grabbed at me and dragged me away.

But these hands didn't belong to the Forest Father.

Chapter Five

I kicked as hard as I could, flailing around wildly. I threw my head back, but nothing worked. They didn't let go. A door opened into a small room, and I was thrust in before the door slammed shut behind me.

I turned to look at the person whose hands had grabbed me, and found a girl, not that much older than myself staring back, breathing heavily.

"Do you always throw yourself around like that?" She muttered, pacing around the room.

"Only when people grab me!" I snapped.

Suddenly another body forced itself into the room, along with a black blur that threw itself against me.

"Skygge!" I gasped, pulling him towards me. His body was shaking from the cold, but he licked my face and sat with his head against my shoulder.

"Who are you?"I demanded, turning my attention to the two girls muttering to each other by the door. The girl who grabbed me was tall, with strong arms and white hair pulled up into an untidy ponytail. The other was about the same height, with caramel skin and dark hair that fell in waves down her slender back, tiny leaves caught between the curling strands.

"We saved your life! And your stupid dog, don't you think you should thank us first?" The blonde girl glared at me, bending to wipe blood from her leg. I hadn't noticed before, but they both looked beaten up.

A long gash ran along the blonde girl's cheek, and the skin had been scraped from her knees.

The dark haired girl was heavily bruised, but she wasn't bleeding like her friend.

"He's not stupid. Don't you know it's rude to talk about people's companions like that?" I glared at her, stroking Skygge comfortingly.

"Companion?" The other girl smirked.

I looked at them, offended but slightly confused.

"Where are your companions?" I sat up straighter, curious to find out who these girls were and why they didn't have their companions with them. After all, they definitely looked old enough to have had their ceremonies already.

"We don't have pets where we come from." One of them said. They were both facing away from me now, looking out of the window into the distance. They whispered, pointing and gesturing.

"He's not a pet!"

"Okay little miss, companion." The blonde girl said, sitting down on the floor opposite me. The blood ran freely down her cheek, and she wiped the back of her hand across it, smearing red.

 "I'm Kara." She thrust her hand out to me, and I shook it.

I wasn't sure if I liked these girls all that much, but they had told me that they saved Skygge, and I was grateful for that. I wiped my hand on my clothes, trying to ignore the blood that was now smeared on it.

 "Loria." The other girl waved a hand at me, still watching the view from the window.

 "Alura…" I told them. "This is Skygge." I gestured at the wet dog leaning against me. I could feel a wet patch forming on my shirt, but I pretended I didn't notice.

His hot breath steamed the air around us, and I stroked his head to calm him. Kara nodded, biting her thumbnail as if she was nervous suddenly. She shifted uncomfortably, peering at Loria from the corner of her eye.

 "You said you don't have companions where you come from…" I didn't make eye contact, the idea of someone not having been put through the ceremonies made me uncomfortable. As far as I was aware, it was custom everywhere, on both sides of the forest.

"Like I said, we don't need them." Loria muttered, turning to us and pulling Kara to her feet.

"But everyone has a companion. You have to!" I argued.

"Not us." Kara huffed, clearly losing her patience. "Now get up little miss, we've got places to be."

Chapter Six

It was hard walking through the forest at night, when the air was misty and you couldn't see your hand in front of your face. The darkness seemed to deepen the further through the woods we walked, and soon I felt smothered.

 "Try and keep up." Kara took my hand, pulling me alongside her. Skygge was following me obediently, rubbing his head against my legs every so often to remind me of his presence.

"How old are you?" Loria asked suddenly, dropping back to walk alongside us.

Her dark hair seemed almost to float around her on the midnight breeze, as if she was underwater.

"Sixteen." I said, knowing that they would have assumed I was younger. "I'm just short."

Loria and Kara exchanged a look that sent a chill down my spine, but I held my head up higher. I didn't want to seem afraid.

"Where are you taking me?" I demanded, stopping short so they had to turn back to face me.

"We're not taking you anywhere." Kara smirked. "We're headed home, but from what we've seen it's safer to bring you with us."

I didn't know what to say to that. A thousand questions buzzed around my mind like tiny bees, caught in a trap.

"You're not kidnapping me?" I asked, still unsure whether I should trust them.

Loria laughed, and Kara nudged her arm. She came closer to me, put her face close to mine, and smiled.

"Do we look like kidnappers to you?" She asked, gesturing from herself to her friend. "If you want to go home, you're free to do so."
I looked around me, the darkness settling in my bones. Skygge was panting softly at my feet, blending into the night. I reached down and buried my hands in his soft coat, the warmth radiating from him and spreading up my arms.
"But I'd recommend you stick with us. It's not safe to be alone right now." Loria frowned, placing a hand on my shoulder.
With what little light that was being cast by the moon, I could just make out their faces. I hadn't noticed how pale Kara was, her hair the colour of fresh snow. She was tall, slim and elegant.
Loria was a complete contrast to her friend, her caramel skin dusted with freckles, her shoulders strong and her legs powerful.
Both had an overwhelming air of strength, beauty and authority about them.
I nodded, following them further into the trees. I thought of my parents, my sisters.

They'd be worried, my father would probably be out looking for me. The Forest Father was sure to tell them what had happened, and they really would think I'd been kidnapped.

"How old are you?" I asked then, and Loria moved to walk next to me.

"Eighteen."

I followed the girls through the trees, the cold wind making me shiver. I wrapped my arms around my chest, trying to keep myself warm. There was a river running down the hill, crystal water rushing against rocks.

Skygge stopped to drink, splashing the dry earth beneath his paws.

"Where are you from?" I asked finally, after what seemed like hours of walking. The two girls seemed nervous to speak, but it was Loria who answered me.

"Have you heard of Willow Hall?" She asked, stepping gracefully over a fallen branch. I fell over it.

"The one from the stories? Where the king sent his daughter?" I snorted.

Everyone knew the stories. The old king had fought for years with his unruly daughter, and on her sixteenth birthday he had banished her from his kingdom and sent her to Willow Hall. Legend said that her unruliness came from her magical gifts. But that was centuries ago, any truth to the story changed slightly with every generation that told it.

"Yes, the one from the stories." Loria glared at me.

"It stood abandoned for many years after the princess, until our people found it." She put an arm around Kara and grinned at me proudly.

"Is that where you're taking me?" I asked, full of sudden wonder at the idea of visiting this magical place. Kara cocked an eyebrow at me, ducking beneath a low hanging branch.

"I told you already, we're going home."

Chapter Seven

The sun was beginning to warm the sky as we
took our first break from walking. How many
hours away from my own home I was, I had no
idea. I didn't want to think about it. Loria had
told me that it was too dangerous to go home
on my own, but taking the safer option meant
leaving my family to worry about me. I
pictured my mother, standing at the window
and crying. My father, trying to console her.
What if he sent the men from the village to
search for me? What if the danger Kara
mentioned caught up with them before it
caught up with us?

I watched birds jump between the branches above our heads. They were small, with sharp talons and brightly coloured feathers. I'd never seen anything like it, and I wondered how many animals lived on this side of the forest that I had never heard of.

A stream ran through the clearing, full of tiny silver fish. I stood over it, watching them shoot from side to side down the stream. When my eyes had become used to the murky water, I noticed larger fish, gold and green. They swam more slowly, relaxed as they let the current pull them down stream.

I sat down on an old tree stump, watching Kara and Loria.

"Why did you tell me the forest is dangerous?" I sipped water from the stream. I cupped my hands and plunged them into the chill water. I was cold already, but it was refreshing.

"The wild creatures are everywhere." Loria replied simply, her attention focused on searching through the pockets of her cloak.

"That's why I have Skygge." I announced proudly, stroking his ears as he sat up attentively. "And that's why you should have companions too."

"We don't have them where we come from. Our people have never had companions." Kara sat down next to me, her long legs crossed elegantly.

She pulled her hair out of her ponytail, and it fell around her like a frosty veil. Her face was the colour of the palest pearl, but her cheeks and nose were pink from the cold.

"But everyone has companions, except…" I started, but Loria cut me off.

She raised her hand in warning, looking around us anxiously. She nodded, and crouched down in front of me.

"You can't just go saying those things." She sighed, shaking her head. "It's not safe."

"But you're…" I stared at her, taking in all of the tiny details I had overlooked before. The golden sparkle of her skin, the honey streaks in her hair, the way she carried herself even in the darkness of the forest at night.

It hadn't really occurred to me that their confidence was unusual. My entire village had a healthy fear of walking alone in the woods, especially at night. But both of these girls seemed completely at home in the darkness, navigating the forest more through touch than sight.

I turned to Kara, who was staring at her feet, her icy hair falling in waves over her shoulders.

She looked up at me and I caught her eyes, blue as the ocean during the Winter Solstice.

Loria looked around us again and after she seemed to decide that it was safe, she held her hand out over a tiny puddle between us. The water began to evaporate, steam rising into the air. I sat staring in shock, my eyes wide.

She smirked and brought her hand up to her face, blowing softly on her palm. The water settled, cooling to its original state.

"That's incredible." I whispered, aware of the look of wonder in my eyes. I turned to Kara, and watched as she placed her pale hand against the ground at our feet.

A few seconds passed, and a tiny shoot appeared in the dirt. A moment later, a small plant was swaying in the breeze, it's leaves unfurling.

"We don't need companions." She looked up at me, "We have our own gifts from the Goddess."

Chapter Eight

We walked miles before the sun began to sink in the sky. Loria said we had to get to higher ground before we set up camp.

 "We don't have anything to sleep under!" I protested, dragging my feet up the mountain behind them. The forest twisted round the mountain, trees snaking along the old path to the other side.

 "It's warm, you don't need anything to sleep under."

 I watched Skygge run ahead, searching our surroundings for any potential threat.

His tail moved frantically from side to side as he sniffed the ground for wild creatures. Eventually he slowed his pace, and made his way back to my side. It had stopped raining properly for the first time in days, patches of earth drying in the last of the sun.

I kicked a loose rock across the path and it skittered away, over the edge of the mountain. I heard it hit branches, leaves, then larger rocks until it fell to the ground below.

"You've never travelled in the wild, have you?" Kara called over her shoulder. I watched her and Loria pointing across the trees, chatting together quietly.

"No, I haven't. Where I come from, we like to keep away from this side of the forest." I admitted, scuffing my feet in the dirt.

"You need to keep quiet, don't draw attention to yourself." She said, nodding towards the edge of the mountain. I frowned, feeling a little embarrassed.

"Sorry." I muttered, hurrying to catch up with them.

...

By the time we reached a tiny clearing in the trees, the sun had disappeared and the moon had taken its place. Stars lit up the sky like tiny gemstones, and I lay beside the fire staring at them.

 "We learned to follow the stars when we were children." Loria told me, pointing out a few constellations.

"Me too, although I've never had to follow them myself." I smiled, staring at the twinkling lights above me.

 "Maybe one day you will." Kara said, laying her cloak out on the grass. She sat down, combing her hair with her fingers. "What does your village look like?" She asked, pausing to turn her attention to me.

Loria stopped toasting nuts on the fire, and moved closer to my spot by the flames.

"I've never seen your village before!" She beamed, eager to hear what my home was like. Kara shot her a warning look, and she smiled at me again, gesturing for me to go on.

"It's pretty small," I shrugged. "Much smaller than Willow Hall must be... there were about twenty or so children in this year's ceremony." I explained.

"What do the houses look like?" They were both listening intently to me now, Loria chewing quietly on the nuts she had already roasted.

"Do you have magic too?"

I snorted. "No, people don't tend to believe in magic anymore. Not where I come from..." I told them. Loria's smile faded.

"Our houses are small, only as big as each family requires. Ours has three rooms. One for my parents and my youngest sister, one for my older sister, and one for me."

"You have sisters?" Loria perked up again, the smile back on her face.

"Lila is youngest, my sister Maure is the eldest."

 "We don't have siblings…" Kara explained, toasting another handful of nuts over the flames. I looked away, suddenly uncomfortable.

 "You have each other…" I said, looking at each of them in turn. "You seem rather like sisters to me!"

 That put a smile on both their faces, and they nodded for me to roast my own food.

 There might not have been much, but I was hungry, and hot food of any kind was welcome. I finished eating, and laid down by the dwindling fire.

 "Get some sleep." Kara told me, "We'll make it home tomorrow if we leave early."

…

I awoke to Loria shaking my shoulders violently. I sat up so quickly I nearly sent her flying across our makeshift camp. She put her finger to her lips before I could ask her what was happening, and held her hand out to me. I took it, my hand too cold and stiff to grasp it properly. I looked around for Kara, but I couldn't see her. It was still dark I realised, it was still night. Loria pulled me towards the edge of the clearing, dragging her feet slowly through the grass and dead leaves.

I copied her, dragging my own bare feet along in her tracks.

The moon was casting shadows across the clearing when I looked over my shoulder. Something rustled the leaves to our right and I gasped, turning to see what it was. Loria clamped her free hand over my mouth, pulling us down into a crouched position.

"Don't make a sound!" She hissed. I nodded weakly, squeezing her hand in mine. We stood up again, and continued dragging our feet along the forest floor.

Suddenly a grey blur shot across in front of us, and Loria threw me behind her. I pressed myself against her back, and tried to keep quiet.

 I could feel her heart beating faster and faster, her breathing ragged. After a few seconds I gathered the courage to peer around her to see what had jumped out at us.

 At first I couldn't see anything, my eyes not accustomed to seeing in the dark. But they adjusted quickly, and I could soon make out the shape of the great wolf pacing in front of us. I closed my eyes, panic consuming me. Loria squeezed my hand, backing away from the wolf as slowly as she could manage with me still behind her.

Before I'd had time to register her, Kara burst out of the trees to our left, swinging a fallen branch at the wolf.

It howled, turning its attention away from us, and stalking slowly towards her.

She nodded at Loria, who ducked down, burying her hands in the soil. The leaves around the wolf's paws started to smoke, and the creature yelped. I gasped, stepping away from Loria to see what was happening.

The sound of my steps on the dry leaves caught the wolf's attention, and I took a deep breath as it began walking towards me. It stopped suddenly, tilting its head as if it was confused. I looked down and noticed vines winding their way around the creatures legs, pinning it to the ground. The vines caught the fire Loria was trying desperately to start, and the creature howled out in pain.

"No!" I screamed, rushing towards it.

"Alura get back! It will kill you!" Kara was sweating, either from the strain of using her magic or from the growing fire.

I ignored her, stepping closer to the wolf, its head swinging around frantically as it tried to understand what was happening.

"Stop, it's scared!" I cried, "It won't hurt us anymore!"

"It's wild!" Loria hissed, staring at me. "Get away from it!"

"It won't hurt us." I repeated, and I placed my hand on the creature's head. The fire went out instantly, as if someone had thrown half the river over it. The vines fell away, and the wolf fell in a heap on the floor. I bent down next to it, my vision blurred by tears. I placed my forehead against it, feeling it's slow but steady breathing.

"It's okay, you're safe now..." I whispered, stroking it's soft coat. I sat there for a while, stroking the injured creature and listening to its heartbeat.

Then it lifted its head, and I lifted my own to look at it. I didn't feel any fear, only an unsettling calmness that I was not used to.

It pushed its nose against my cheek and stood up, before running off in the direction it had come from.

Chapter Nine

"How did you know how to do that?" Kara demanded, her arms crossed against her sweat-soaked tunic. She was still breathing heavily, pacing in front of me. Loria was staring at me, as if I was from another world.

"I don't know!" I sighed, for the hundredth time. "I just did it. I know it was dangerous, I'm sorry..."

"No." Kara grabbed my shoulders.

"Don't be sorry." Loria shook her head. "You don't understand, do you?" She asked, her eyes shining.

"No, I don't." I moaned, the reality of what I'd done suddenly hitting me. It should have killed me. I should have been scared. But I felt its fear. I felt how scared and vulnerable it was. It's emotions consumed me, seeping into my soul until I felt them too. Loria and Kara seemed to be arguing, their backs turned towards me, but eventually Kara pulled me down to sit with her on a fallen tree.

"Have you heard of anyone who had a creature like your Skygge as a companion?" Kara asked, a subtle smile playing on her lips.

"Only the King's daughter, but that was part of the legend. She had magic, she didn't need a Companion, did she?" I shook my head.

"It's not just that we don't need them Alura..." Loria sighed, joining us on the tree.

"The Goddess doesn't give us companions. Do you know what happens when children go missing in the woods during their rituals?"

I nodded, then thought about it and shook my head. I'd never asked.

When children went missing, we were too frightened to ask what happened to them, where they'd gone.

 "We take those children to Willow Hall. It's not safe for them to be on your side of the forest. They aren't allocated a companion by the Goddess. They have gifts just like we do." She explained. I didn't understand. It didn't make sense. I had a companion, he was sitting right in front of me. "We have to learn to use our gifts to protect us."

 "The only companion gifted children are ever allocated, are creatures like Skygge." She nodded at the dog sitting at my feet, staring up at me as if he was transfixed by my face.

 "That's why we took you from your village Alura." Loria explained, placing her hand on mine. "We had to keep you safe.
You could blend in with the other villagers for a time, you have a companion. But it wouldn't last long, and someone would learn of your gifts."

I stared into the distance, my whole body tense as I tried to take in what was happening.

"Are there many different gifts people are given?" I asked, dragging my feet in the dirt.

"Ours are quite unusual, that's why we are often sent to retrieve newly gifted children." Kara explained proudly.

"A few can freeze the air with their touch, others can burn things with their mind..." Loria said thoughtfully.

My own mind was spinning at the thought, my heart pounding.

"How many people are there at Willow Hall?" I whispered, trying to imagine a village full of people with such incredible gifts.

"Less than there have been before." was all Kara replied, standing up.

"We have other ways to keep ourselves safe." Kara smirked, her eyes gleaming. She could sense my discomfort, and changed the subject. I was grateful for it.

Drawing a small sword from under her cloak, she held it out in front of her.

"How long have you had that?" my eyes widened. The idea that she had been hiding a weapon on her the whole time we had been wandering the forest seemed unbelievable to me.

I'd never seen someone with a weapon before, the villagers at home had no use for them, other than axes for chopping wood.

"Since we left Willow Hall to find you." She replied slyly. She held it out for me to take, and I took in the feel of the cold metal against my skin. It was heavier than I had expected, an even weight in my hand.

"You should learn how to fight." Loria announced, drawing her own sword.

I laughed again. "You'll learn how to conceal a weapon without accidentally stabbing yourself, don't worry."

"You hold it like this..." Loria braced herself, keeping the sword across her body. "To protect yourself. Deflect the other persons attack."

Kara swung her sword out, and Loria caught it with the edge of her blade. I nodded.

"You try."

I held the sword out, trying to copy Loria's stance. Kara swung her own sword, and narrowly missed my left arm. She smirked.

"You'll learn fast enough." She slapped me on the back and took her sword back. "We can practice more when we get to Willow Hall"

Chapter Ten

The next few hours seemed to blur together. We started hiking further up the mountain towards the other side of the forest. We reached a point where the trees became a wall in front of us, the thick branches heavy with snow. Loria shivered beside me, her cloak wrapped tightly around her shoulders. A light layer of snow settled on her hair, making it glisten in the sun.

Kara walked ahead steadily, her head held high.

You could tell from her shaking hands that she was just as cold as we were, but she refused to show it.

I kicked the snow away, forcing a path ahead for myself as I moved through the forest, flakes falling softly from the pearly sky.

"From here we go down." Kara announced, edging her way through the pines and down the dirt path. I followed obediently, Skygge close behind me.

We walked until my feet were blistered, and my legs aching. I'd heard stories of what lay on the other side of the forest, but I'd never thought I'd see it for myself. There were different plants, tall ones with brightly coloured flowers, and trees with fruit I'd never seen before. The sun rose and fell in the sky before we came to the edge of the forest. Their side of the forest.

"We're here!" Loria beamed, throwing her arms wide and ushering me up a small stone path. More pine trees grew on either side, but smaller and fresher than those in the forest. We soon realised though, that something was very, very wrong.

A boy, a few years older than me came rushing down the path towards us.

He ran straight past me, ignoring Skygge and grabbed Kara by the shoulders. Before he could say anything, she eyed me closely and pulled him away so I couldn't hear them. I watched her face grow pale, even more than usual. She lowered her head as the boy began shouting, his words becoming more and more frantic. Suddenly she shushed him, nodding and taking his arm in hers. She walked towards me, Loria keeping close to my side. I looked around at the village we had arrived in.

Willow Hall itself stood proudly in the centre, its silver-grey stone shining in the pale light. Around it, huts were clustered between burned out fires. But there were no people outside. Nobody selling food, nobody lighting fires to cook. I swallowed hard, taking in the eerie quietness of the empty village.

There was a larger hut at the edge of the village, with smoke rising from a fire outside the door. A wave of relief rolled over me.

People. It was a short lived feeling though, as I turned to see Kara striding towards me, her fists balled at her sides.

"Alura, Harker will take you to the main hall. Loria and I have some urgent business to attend to. Wait for us there and we will come for you as soon as we can." Kara took Loria's hand, and the two of them marched off together, towards the huts and away from me.

I felt panic rise up in my heart. They couldn't just leave me, not with a stranger. The boy, Harker, looked at me uncomfortably.

"You'd better come with me then." He said, gesturing for me to follow.

The path to the hall was overgrown with vines, and I took my time stepping over them as Harker stormed ahead. I looked up at the building ahead of me, taking in the sheer size of it.

The sound of metal hitting stone poured out through an open window, and I waited behind Harker as he climbed the steps to the old wooden door.

Chapter Eleven

The hall was hidden deep within the trees. Mist swirled around us like an ocean, and I watched Harker knock rhythmically on the door. After a few seconds, a man in a dark cloak peered around the door as it creaked open. He took one look at me and raised his weapon. Harker threw his hands towards the man, shaking his head.

 "She came with Kara." Harker told him, and whispered something as the man locked eyes with me. He grunted, opening the door just wide enough for us to squeeze through.

Harker gestured to the rows of wooden chairs lining the cold stone walls. I sat in a corner, Skygge by my feet.

He was panting softly, rubbing his face against my legs. Soon he sat up, watching the others closely. His eyes narrowed as someone moved closer.

"How'd you come to on this side of the forest?" The man in the dark cloak sat a few chairs away, swinging his heavy arms onto his lap.

"Kara and Loria brought me here. They said I wasn't safe. Someone attacked me while I was visiting…" I paused. Things were different here, and I didn't want to give away too much about where I came from. "A friend." I finished. The man looked at me skeptically, rubbing his beard with fat fingers and leaning forward in his seat.

"Who attacked you?" He raised an eyebrow. His face was hard and stern, his hair dark and cropped short, framing his features perfectly. He was strong and fierce, but I wouldn't let him frighten me.

"I don't know." I shook my head. The man frowned at me, and opened his mouth to say something, but was cut off by the doors swinging open and Kara bursting in.

"We have to leave." She announced, striding across the room and grabbing me by my wrist. I snatched it back, looking around at the unfamiliar faces staring back at me.

"Leave. Leave and go where?" I asked, crossing my thin arms across my chest, trying to sound braver than I felt.

"North. To the Forge, we need to get to higher ground.

It'll be safer." Kara sighed, collecting things from around the room into a large leather bag. She threw it over her shoulder and looked up at me desperately.

"Safer than what? What are we hiding from?" I sank down into my chair again, the older man a few seats away following me with his intense eyes.

Kara rubbed her temples with her thumbs. She took a few steps towards me, and put her hands on my shoulders.

"Someone like you."

Time seemed to stop.

"Like me?" I frowned. "You mean, my people? Are they coming to find me?" Kara shook her head, her white hair flying around her face.

"Someone who can do what you do. Someone who can talk to the wild creatures." Kara explained, searching my eyes for an understanding.

"You're like her?" The man demanded, standing up and pointing his sword at me with shaking arms. Loria rushed over, standing between us.

"She's not like anyone Draga." She snapped. He huffed and slumped back into his chair, but his sword remained in his hands, ready to attack at any moment.

"We need to go." Kara repeated, nodding towards the door. Her leather bag was overflowing now, bulging with knives and herbs and anything she could find that might be of some use later on. Loria gave me a half hearted smile, and held out her hand to me. I took it, standing up on shaking legs and following her to the door.

"Draga, I need you to round up the others. Anyone who's left." Kara was saying, directing Draga around the hall.

"Who is it?" I whispered to Loria, hoping nobody would hear us talking. We huddled together by the door, our voices low.

"Her name is Eslanda. She came from the same village as Kara." Loria explained.

"She didn't return from her ritual, but our people could not find her. She spent a long time wandering the forest alone, fighting to stay alive."

"And that made her bitter." Kara came up behind us, sliding an axe through her belt. "She thought at first that our people abandoned her. Now she has grown arrogant, and believes they feared her."

"Why would they fear her?" I asked, trying to imagine a whole village of people, gifted like Loria and Kara were. I couldn't picture them being frightened of a little girl.

"Because the goddess granted her the rarest of abilities." Loria frowned. "Her own ability; to control the wild creatures."

I sucked in a breath. Skygge was sitting at my feet. He appeared relaxed, but I could feel the tension in his muscles as he remained alert, constantly searching for danger.

"Did your people ever find her?" I looked around the room at the few villagers inside the hall. Draga was talking to one woman as she packed herbs into her bag.
Her hair was dark and curly, her skin the colour of the moon.

"Yes, but she refused to go with them. She lives alone in the forest." Kara handed me a small knife, and I looked at the cold metal as it reflected the light coming through the windows. "She swore revenge on us all for abandoning her through fear and selfishness."

The look in her pale eyes as she spat the word revenge unnerved me. She sounded both furious and terrified, and I didn't like it.

Chapter Twelve

Forty six.

There were forty six people left in the village.
Kara's eyes were empty of any emotion, but
Loria's spilled hot tears down her cheeks. I sat
beside Harker as he counted the villagers one
last time.

 'All right.' He nodded to Kara, and she took up
her bag. Swinging it over her shoulder, she
slipped her sword into its sheath at her waist,
and signalled for me to follow her.

I stood up, my legs threatening to give way
beneath me.

My fingers clutched the knife Kara had given me, and I eyed the people milling around outside the hall.

They were split into two groups, and I watched Loria lead the first group down the old path away from the hall. She had handed me a bundle of cloth, and I unravelled it to find a cloak and a small bag filled with herbs. I pulled the cloak around me, the thick grey fabric warm against my frozen skin.

"We need to find those that fled. We have a safe place in the North, they'll have headed there." Kara told me, her arms folded across her body. She looked down at Skygge and gave me a half hearted smile. The second group consisted of mainly children, and they huddled around me and Skygge. One of the children buried her hands into his soft fur, looking up and me in wonder.

"You're from far away." She whispered, her eyes wide.

I smiled, "Very far away."

Kara started up the path where the first group had vanished ahead of us, and I followed her with the children walking behind me.

I wondered how many had fled. How many people there would be in total.

I could tell it worried Kara, as she counted heads from the corner of her eye. She was concerned about losing more.

I wrapped my cloak tighter around my shoulders, shielding myself from the cool wind. Kara was marching ahead, her hand on the sword at her hip, eyeing the forest suspiciously.

The moon made its way higher into the night sky, casting flickering shadows onto the grassy path. Families huddled together further down the path, closer to the front of the group.

The children huddled close to their parents, holding hands and clinging to cloaks. I wondered how many times they'd been this deep into the forest before.

I was too busy watching the villagers around me to notice that Kara had stopped ahead, and was setting up a shelter in a clearing. She hung a lantern from a low hanging branch, and started on some smaller shelters. I hurried to help, pulling blankets and lanterns from the bags people had carried away from Willow Hall.

The moon stared down at us through a gap in the trees, stars freckling the midnight sky. Parents tucked children under blankets, and everyone gathered around the fire where Kara sat with Harker, Loria and Draga.

Draga was a large man, all wide shoulders and thick muscles. Beside him, Harker was spindly legs and a narrow chest, his arms not much bigger than mine.

He had a stern face though, and a voice much louder than you'd expect. For such a small man, he oozed authority. Draga on the other hand had an air of arrogance, but also of fear. The fire cracked in the middle of the camp, providing the only warmth we had.

"How much further?" An elderly man growled from beside the flames. His wife sat beside him, her white hair in a tangled braid down her back.

"It is hard to tell in the dark Garl." Loria sighed, rubbing her temples. "I should think maybe half a days walk." Heavy sighs and muttered arguments rumbled through the crowd of villagers gathered in the clearing.

"What if we're attacked?"

"What if the wild creatures come?"

A wave of people surged towards Kara as she tried to calm the situation. I looked around, counting the faces of those still awake and wondering how they would manage to walk so far without stopping.

Many of the villagers travelling with us were older, and those who weren't had small children to worry about. They spent most of their time carrying infants as they walked the long journey, trying to keep up. Long breaks during the day would draw out the wild creatures, it wasn't safe.

"If the wild creatures attack we will defend ourselves." Harker shouted, standing up to the crowd. "We have weapons."

"We are not warriors." A tall, dark man stood forward. "And our gifts are not the kind that would help defend us against this threat."

Loria scoffed. "Of course they are." She reached her hand out to a pile of dead leaves sitting against the trunk of an old tree,

and a fire erupted outward, sending golden sparks into the air.

"We will build defences tonight." She announced, "and destroy them tomorrow. Cover our tracks."

Kara stood up, her black cloak swirling around her feet in the night breeze. She threw her hands up, and tiny shoots appeared, circling the encampment. She struggled, forcing them to grow faster. Her arms shook under the weight of her magic, but she strained against it. It took her a long time, but she had built up a wall of branches, enclosing the camp from the rest of the forest.

"Isha!" She cried, stumbling back. A small, dark haired girl ran forward, reaching for Kara.

She pulled her hand away, nodding at the wall of leaves surrounding us. Isha took a deep breathe, looking around nervously. "Go ahead."

Isha turned to the branches, and blew a soft breath onto the leaves.

Flakes of frost spread through the night air, and the branches froze into solid ice before our eyes. Isha stepped back warily, pulling her hand back to her side. She rubbed it against her clothes, warming it.

"We will be protected for the night." Loria called out. "Sleep, rest. We leave at sunrise."

Chapter Thirteen

I woke just before the sun rose, peeling myself from my blanket and staring around the camp. The gentle crack of melting ice drew my attention to Loria, as she held her hand against the frozen wall that encircled us. Steam filled the cold air, making it difficult for me to see as I stumbled towards her. My feet were cold and stiff, and I rubbed my hands together under my cloak as I stood beside Loria at the edge of camp.

Looking round, I could see a few others working on the ice too.

"Kara was right." She smiled, her eyes still focused on the frozen branches.

"Half a days walk and we'll reach the Forge, and the rest of our people."

I nodded, looking around at the rest of the villagers as they rose from their sleep. Children sat by small fires, rubbing their eyes sleepily as they played together. I spotted Kara by the main fire in the centre of the camp, her white hair twisted into a loose bun on top of her head.

She was talking to Harker, her face stern and serious. She took a copper pot from the fire, spooning soup into small bowls and handing them to the children and the elderly.

"Kara makes a good leader." I said, turning back to Loria.

The ice had melted now, and I wondered how long she had been here, her hands turning our wall into nothing more than a giant puddle. She held out her hand again, steam rising from the ground. The puddle evaporated before my eyes.

A small boy, no older than ten came out of the shadows. Loria bent to his level and smiled at him.

"Ren, this is Alura." She gestured at me, and the boy blushed.

"It's nice to meet you Ren." I told him, offering him my hand to shake.

He looked at it for a while, as if he was expecting something. Loria laughed, ushering him forward to shake it.

"Why don't you show Alura what you can do Ren? Don't be shy." She put her hand on his shoulder, and he beamed proudly.

Stepping forward, he stared at the wall of branches in front of us.

For a moment, I was confused, until I noticed his blue eyes turn to the colour of flames. The bushes burst into light, flaming and burning to the ground in an instant. I gaped at the small boy beside me. How could someone so small, so young, do something like that? He turned to me, his eyes burning sapphire again, and his face warm like he'd been caught by a summer sun.

"Do you have a gift?" He asked, stepping closer to me.

"I..." I started, but Loria cut me off.

"We will be leaving soon Ren, you should find your parents. Thank you for your help."
She ruffled his hair, nudging him softly in the direction he'd come from.

"For now Alura, I'd keep your gifts secret." She whispered, linking her arm through mine and heading towards Kara. "Until we know its safe."

"How do the children here have gifts?" I asked, "They're not old enough to have taken part in a ceremony." I looked over to Ren, his childlike features highlighted by the flickering flames.

"Some people inherit them. It's unusual, but it happens. Most children here are not gifted, but they travel with us all the same. They are family."

The sun was high in the sky above our heads, and we'd been walking for hours. We were following a small stream, heading further into the woods. My mind buzzed with thoughts of my family. My mother would be beside herself with worry, my sisters too.

My father was probably out searching, most likely with other men from the village. Then my thoughts went to the Forest Father. What had happened to him that day? Where had he gone when Kara and Loria had taken me with them to Willow Hall?

Kara was a few steps ahead of me, talking to Draga and Harker as they sharpened their knives.

While they walked towards the front of the group, I was left behind with the children. I'd asked Kara whether it was safe for me to be at the back, leaving the children quite unprotected, but she had only told me to stop worrying. That should danger catch up with us, they would be safe.

"Kara!" I called, hurrying a little to match her stride. Her legs were strong and athletic, she was used to walking like this. Instinctively, she swung around, her sword in her hand before I had even finished calling her name. I put my hands up, showing her that everything was okay.

"I just wanted to talk." I told her, and she relaxed into herself again.

Her sword slipped back into its sheath, and she put an arm around me.

"About what?"

"The day you came for me... What happened to the Forest Father?" I asked, watching her face twist with a look of confusion. She thought for a second.

"The old man?"

"He was trying to keep me quiet, hide me." I said, and she nodded.

"He went back inside once he realised who we were. He knew we were taking you to safety." She explained. "We've met him before." My eyes went wide.

"You've met him before? The Forest Father?"

"Sure. Most children gifted by the Goddess come with us, so we travel to many villages to take them to the safety of Willow Hall."

"Haven't you ever wondered where the missing children went?" Harker interrupted, and I straightened. I hadn't known that he'd been listening.

"We were always told that… that they didn't make it." I said, and his eyebrow twitched. "That they were dead."

Harker scoffed, "Nice lot in your village. Telling little children their friends are dead."

Kara shot him a fierce look, and his eyes dropped to the ground.

"A lot of people are scared of magic these days. It's not unusual for children to be told that." She frowned, squeezing my shoulder.

"Are they all here? With your people I mean?" I grinned at the idea of my fallen friends being alive, not just alive- but gifted!

"Many of them." Kara confirmed. "Some refuse to come with us, but we have people who watch out for them from time to time. You'll be able to see the ones who came with us once we reach the Forge."

Chapter Fourteen

Screaming.

Everything had been quiet, so quiet.
Unnaturally quiet. It was as if the forest itself
had fallen asleep. The group had begun to slow
as the children got tired, and the only sound I
was aware of was the leaves rustling in the
trees. But then there was screaming. Hard,
desperate screaming that cut right through
you.

When it stopped, my heart was pounding in my
chest as I searched the faces around me for
Kara.

"Stay together!" She yelled, motioning for us to huddle in the centre of the path.

She ran a little way into the trees and dropped down into the tall grass. She shook something on the ground and stood up again, a raw growl escaping her body as she turned to us. Blood coated her hands, trickling down her arms. It dripped from her fingers and pooled at her feet. I stopped breathing, waiting for her to say something, but she didn't.

She stared around her angrily, her face almost as red as the blood on her hands.

Loria ran over to her, and whispered something before they both drew their weapons and came back towards the group.

"Does everyone able to fight have a weapon?" Loria called out, staring into the faces of all the villagers gathered in the forest. Nobody spoke. She nodded. "Good."

Suddenly, another scream came from the back of the group. I spun around, my whole body shaking. Kara sprinted towards me, grabbing my arm and dragging me with her towards the other side of the path.

"I need your help." She whispered, pulling me to face her. I tried to look behind her, but she lifted my face up to look into her eyes.

"You are our greatest weapon Alura." She hissed.

She let me go, and I saw Loria kneeling on the ground. She was staring into the woods, her sword clutched tight in her hand beside her.

A trail of fresh blood ran from her feet, into the woods ahead of us.

She turned to me, and I knew what she was asking. I nodded reluctantly, although I knew I had no choice. I heard a woman crying, her sobs echoing through the trees. I drew my sword and held it up in front of me, and followed both girls into the forest.

I tried to ignore the smell of blood as we climbed over the limbs of fallen trees. Skygge stuck close by me, so quiet I barely knew he was here. He sniffed around frantically, his nose so low it dragged across the ground. I watched him from the corner of my eye as we continued, still following the thin trail of blood.

Loria stopped just ahead of me, her hand thrown back to halt us.

She crouched down, her eyes focused ahead as she signalled for us to approach.

Just in front of us, beside a small ditch sat a wolf, larger than any I'd seen before, or had even heard about. It's grey fur rippled as it moved, pacing around the body it had dropped at its feet. I held my breath, trying not to cry out. But the animal sat calmly, looking down at the body curiously.

It nudged the face with its huge wet nose, rubbing its head against it. Kara turned to me, her eyes red and swollen.

I stepped past her, and the wolf tore its attention away from the body it was studying so intently.

I watched, my fists clenched at my sides as the animal strode towards me. I forced my breathing to slow, taking long deep breaths as it stared at me with its amber eyes.

"Be careful." Loria warned from where she crouched below the grass with Kara. I didn't move, my attention still focused on the wolf.

It came towards me faster, and I gasped, closing my eyes. It would attack me, I was sure of it.

But Skygge sat patiently at my side, watching the creature move. When I peeled my eyes open, the wolf was sat facing me.

I dragged in a deep breath, shuffling forward in the dead leaves at my feet. I reached my hand up warily, slowly moving it towards the huge wolf.

Its head was easily three times the size of Skygge's, and my palm rested gently between its eyes.

I felt a warm heat surge through my fingers, and the wild creature's eyes seemed to flicker. It bowed its head slightly, and I pulled my hand back, resting it cautiously on my sword. The wolf tilted its head at Skygge, and something seemed to pass between them. Kara stood nervously, her arm linked into Loria's.

 I smiled, turning triumphantly towards them.

 "He is safe." I said, nodding towards the wolf. They didn't look convinced, but Kara gave me a quick smile and nodded.

 Then her eyes fell onto the body on the ground, as a sputtering sound burst into the air.

She flew past me, falling onto her knees and lifting the woman into her arms.

 "She's alive!" She cried to Loria, who rushed to sit beside her. She pulled out some herbs and a few strips of fabric from her bag, and set to work bandaging the woman's wounds. Kara held the woman still, whispering to her softly.

 "We will have Shari see to her?" Loria asked quietly, and Kara nodded. I watched as the two of them carried the woman back towards the path, Skygge and the wolf standing silently beside me.

Chapter Fifteen

The Forge was a large, dark wooden building, set in a clearing at the top of the mountain. Its windows were small and boxy, letting in little light from the afternoon sun. Kara had carried the injured woman in through the back of the Forge, and set her on a table where a young girl began treating her properly.

"Is she the only casualty?" A tall man with pale hair and a scruffy beard leaned against the table.

Kara flinched, and I remembered her face as we burned the body of the dead villager, her hands clasped together solemnly as Ren set fire to the pile of branches we had placed them on.

"No Kar. We lost one other." Kara admitted. Her hair was pulled back from her face, but a few loose strands stuck to her face. The man frowned, his eyebrows scrunching together in the middle of his forehead.

"She will survive." Loria confirmed, drying her hands on a scrap of fabric. She dropped it onto the table as a few other villagers helped the woman down and led her out of the room.

"I don't think it was a vicious injury." Kara sighed, catching my eye as she spoke to Kar. He glared at me, rubbing his beard as he thought things over in his mind. He knew.

"The wound being on the lower leg suggests it was from dragging rather than mauling." Loria agreed, standing beside me.

Kar looked at her suspiciously, before brushing past me and walking out the door.

"Don't mind him." Kara rolled her eyes, clearing up the herbs and old bandages Loria had discarded on the table.

"Who is he?" I asked, looking over my shoulder to see him standing just through the doorway, talking to Draga.

"My brother." Kara sighed, sitting on a stool by the window. "We're not very close."

Loria scoffed. "He was the same age as Eslanda when she refused to come with us." She told me, "He was... in love with her." At that, Kara laughed and looked away.

"He was a child." She muttered, "We all were."

She turned her attention to the indoor herb garden on the windowsill. The boxes of dirt were empty of any plants, but Kara buried her hand in the earth and watched tiny shoots grow between her fingers.

...

Harker burst in, his face red and dripping with sweat. Wherever he'd run from, it can't have been nearby.

"What's the matter?" Kara asked, seeming uninterested in Harker's urgency. He gulped down a breath, his hands on his knees as he doubled over to catch his breath.

"Isha" he coughed. "She's missing!" Kara's face turned stony as she looked past Harker into the hallway. She pushed past him, and Loria pulled a face at me across the room.

We followed Kara as she headed towards the front door. Outside, the air was cold and the gathering of people sent a chill down my spine. A woman grabbed Kara's shoulders, sobbing and shaking. Kara pulled the woman to her, letting her cry onto her shoulder. She looked over at me quickly, and I watched as she held the woman's face gently but firmly as she spoke to her.

"I will find her." She promised, and the woman tried to smile. The curve of her lips fell as her desperate face searched the gathering crowd.

I watched as Harker returned with weapons, which he slid into a large bag and slung over Kara's shoulder.

"You'll take my horse." He said, and Kara nodded. She came over to Loria and I, and a look passed between the two of them that I could not understand. "You are in charge in my place." She told Loria, who bit her lip but stood up a little straighter.

"You are more than capable." Kara turned to me next, and smiled. "You will protect the villagers, but most importantly Loria." She said.

"Harker will be in charge of any fighting that may occur. If you are attacked, use your gifts but listen to Harker. Do as he says if they come for you." I looked at my feet.

I didn't know what I was doing, I was new to their world. She lifted my chin, and I forced myself to smile reassuringly.

"Ready?" Harker called, and handed the reins to Kara. She took the horse and Draga helped her up, leading her down the path.

"He will see her as far as she allows him to." Loria whispered, turning and starting towards the Forge. She stopped after a few steps, turning and waiting for me to join her.

Skygge waited patiently at the front door, watching me intently. He had taken to staying a few steps behind me wherever I went, but he never took his full attention from me.

"We will wait for her return. Then we move on." Loria spoke nervously, unsure of her position now that Kara had left her in charge.

"Where will we go? Can we not stay here?" I asked, confused. Hadn't we come here for safety? Wasn't that why we had come here?

"We can't stay in one place too long. Eslanda will catch word of where we are and she will come for us." Loria shook her head, her dark hair flicking around her face.

I followed her into the Forge, up a set of steps and into a small room at the back of the building. It overlooked the forest, the river running along the opposite side of the building. She dropped her cloak onto a chair.

"You can stay with me." She motioned to the two single beds pushed to either side of the room.

"I need an advisor, and I don't like the idea of having to listen to Harker's every word. Power goes straight to his head." She rolled her eyes. I laughed.

Chapter Sixteen

Almost a week had passed, and there was still no sign of Kara. If she did not return in within two days, Loria said we would be forced to leave without her.

 I spent the majority of my time training with Harker. His preferred weapon was an axe, and he tried desperately to teach me how to use one. It was still early in the morning, and the sun was barely visible over the horizon.

I was wearing thick wool trousers, and an embroidered tunic that Loria had lent me. They were both too large for me, but they were warm.

Loria sat by the side of the field, her ocean blue dress catching the sunlight. She was flipping through the pages of a huge leather bound book, scribbling notes onto a piece of paper beside her.

"Pay attention." Harker snapped, drawing my attention back as he swung his axe at my head. I ducked, rolling to the side and finding my feet a few feet away from him. He looked at me.

"When you roll, you move away from your enemy, not towards them." He raised an eyebrow. I was reaching to slap the smile from his face when Loria cleared her cleared her throat across the field.

"Alura, would you come with me to the Hall?" She called, her eyes flicking between Harker and I.

Wiping my forehead with the back of my hand, I nodded, glaring at Harker before following her down the path.

...

"I don't know how much more of him I can take." I mumbled.

Loria smirked, "I did warn you."

We continued down the path until we reached the back gates to the hall. Draga stood guarding them, his heavy arms crossed against his chest.

An axe hung from his belt, and a sword stood up against the wall beside him. He nodded at us each in turn, before opening the gates and letting us walk past, his eyes following me suspiciously.

There was a small room just before the entrance to the main hall, which appeared to be most frequently used as a meeting room. Books lined every wall, and a large oak table sat in the centre. On it lay maps, piles of loose papers, and wax for sealing letters. I looked around in wonder. Loria sat heavily in on of the chairs, pulling herself closer to the table. I sat next to her, watching as she tucked her own papers under one of the piles.

"Kara's father has been Watcher here for as long as anyone remembers." Loria told me. "But now he is old, and frail."

"And Kara must take on his role." I nodded, understanding.

"Kar refuses, and Kara has no choice." Loria sighed.

I could see the pain in her eyes as she thought of what was to come.

The Watcher has many responsibilities in any village, but I couldn't imagine what it would entail here.

Every village has an allocated Watcher; someone to protect and control the ordinary folk. They create the laws, and it is their job to ensure they are followed.

"He named his son Kar, as it means 'victorious'. But when Kara was born, the Watcher wanted to edge his bets. He named her victorious too." She laughed, but there was no humour in it.

I had thought it strange that their names were so similar, but had assumed that maybe it was common on this side of the forest. Most villages had their own naming customs, usually to name the first born son after their father.

"You live so differently here..." I smiled. She glanced over at me, her face drawn. I wondered how much sleep she'd had since Kara left.

"We have our ways. They like to think of Willow Hall as the last kingdom. Even though the princess is well and truly dead."

...

That afternoon, Loria and I visited Kara's father.

The Watcher had remained to protect his land, even when only a few had remained alongside him. He had a small house behind the main hall, quiet and hidden. Ivy framed the old wooden door, set into the cold stone walls.

Smoke rose from the chimney, blending into the stormy sky above us.

Loria creaked the door open, calling out into the dark hallway. A mumble drifted from inside and Loria pushed her way in, gesturing for me to follow her.

"What's his name?" I stopped her, and she looked at me strangely, as if she had forgotten that I had only just arrived here.

"Nobody knows." She shrugged. "I just call him Sir."

I followed Loria into the living room and stood by the fire, letting its warmth seep into my bones. Kara's father sat in a worn armchair by the window, his feet up on a wooden stool. He lifted his head as we entered, and grinned at Loria. His eyes were dark and thoughtful, and his untamed white hair framed his thin face in gentle, messy waves.

"Sir, this is Alura." She took his hand, nodding towards me. I shifted uncomfortably. Skygge sat obediently by my feet, his breathing quiet and his eyes focused on the old man.

"A wolf!" The Watcher cried, trying to sit up. I gasped, rushing forward to calm him.

"No wolf Sir." I shook my head, "He is my companion." I reassured him, and Loria pulled a chair from the corner of the room to sit beside Kara's father.

"A companion?" He smirked skeptically, squinting at me closely. "You bring the ordinary folk here now?" He looked at Loria and she laughed.

"No Sir. She is one of us."

The old man pushed himself up enough to look me straight in the eyes.

"So tell me," he whispered. "If you are indeed one of us, and you have a companion... are you here to save us?"

I searched Loria's face for any help as to how I should answer. Was I here to save them? I was still just a child, barely sixteen.

I knew nothing of their world.

"She will help us fight against Eslanda." Loria stood up, nodding to Kara's father as he stared at me.

His eyes drifted slowly over to Skygge, who remained by the fire.

"It's been a long time since I met someone with a companion." He smiled, holding his hand out to me. "And much longer since someone has had a companion such as this."

I took his hand. "I will do what I can to save your people." I told him, lowering my eyes in embarrassment. How could I save anyone?

He let go of my hand, bringing his own up to raise my chin. He smiled, his eyes bright as stars.

"Our people."

Chapter Seventeen

"We must leave." Loria shook me awake, her hair falling over her face as she bent over my bed. I sat up, rubbing my eyes and trying to comprehend the situation. A large leather bag lay open on Loria's bed, and she was packing clothes into it hurriedly.

"Kara! Is she..." I jumped up from my bed, rushing towards Loria.

"No." She shook her head, "she has not returned." I looked at my feet.

"The wild creatures attacked last night." Loria explained, rubbing her forehead.

"Nobody was killed, but the guards were injured."

I shifted uncomfortably, not knowing how to help. "Can I help pack?"

Loria smiled at me sympathetically, and handed me a leather pouch. "There are herbs in the healing room."

The healing room was damp, and much colder than the rest of the Hall. I lit a candle in the corner of the room, and brought it with me to the windowsill. A pair of small iron scissors lay on the side, and I snipped a handful of each herb, placing them carefully in the pouch.

I collected some bandages, folding the neatly and tucking them under my arm, and followed the steps back up towards Loria's room. Something caught my eye as I reached the top of the stairs, and I turned to see Draga watching me from the end of the hallway.

He strode towards me, his steps powerful and deliberate. He stood so close to me that I had to take a step back, gripping the handrail to stop me toppling down the stairs.

He opened his mouth to say something, his eyes slits as he glared at me. The the door swung open and Loria came towards me.

"Thank you Alura..." she turned to Draga, her eyes low and threatening. "Can we help you Draga?"

"No." He growled, glaring at us both as he made his way down the stairs. I looked helplessly at Loria and she frowned.

"Ignore him." She waved a hand in the direction of the stairs, and ushered me through the door. "He's probably just worried about Kara."

I wasn't sure if I believed her, but there wasn't a whole lot I could do, so I tried to forget about it.

I handed the pouch of herbs to Loria, her warm hands clasping the leather.

"Do you know much about healing?" She asked, sitting on a stool by the window. I shook my head, sitting on my bed and watching her pull one of the bundles of herbs out. She held it in front of her, studying the leaves. Then they shrivelled, drying right there before my eyes. She placed them carefully back in the pouch, and added it to the bag on her bed.

 "I will ask Shari to teach you." She offered, "When all this is over."

It was midday when we finally set out, and the sun was hot and bright on our backs as we headed further North. I carried my cloak, the heat too much to bare it. Loria was leading the group, her dark hair braided loosely down her back.

Her cloak was a light linen, draped over her shoulders and cascading around her like waterfall.

 I had been charged with watching the children again, and I walked slowly so they could keep up. Skygge marched alongside me proudly, watching the children from the corner of his emerald eyes. A little girl pushed through the crowd of children to reach my side, and held up what at first I thought was some kind of precious stone.

"How beautiful!" I smiled, impressed with her find. She giggled as the stone fell onto my palm and I gasped, almost dropping it. "It's cold!"

"It's ice!" She beamed at me, scooping up water from a puddle at the edge of the path and freezing it in her hands. She shaped it with her fingers and held it up for me to see.

"Well, that certainly is impressive!" I told her, and she blushed.

"I can kill things." A small voice came from behind me, and I almost cried out. How horrific!

"Nobody wants to see your gift, it's horrible!" Another voice snapped and I turned to see two boys staring back at me. Their eyes were very deep blue, like berries.

"No, no. I want to see your gift." Of course I didn't, it sounded morbid. "As long as you don't kill any of us…"

The boy smirked and threw his hand towards a patch of wildflowers, and I watched as they wilted and fell down into the soil. The boy standing next to him rolled his eyes and flicked a finger at the dead plants, sticking his tongue out mockingly as the flowers grew healthy and beautiful again in an instant.

"We're the twins." The first boy nodded at his brother, his face like thunder.

"You're certainly very talented." I said, trying to sound reassuring. Frankly they both frightened me.

"What can you do?" The ice girl asked, stepping forward again. I remembered Loria's warnings.

"We're not sure yet." I said, only half lying. I certainly felt like I had no idea.

Chapter Eighteen

We'd not walked far, a few miles at the most. It was still light, the sun low in the sky, but still there. Loria had positioned Harker, Draga and the three other guards from Willow Hall around the group, protecting us as we travelled. It was one of the three guards I had not met yet that brought the news.

"I see her!" He yelled, and it felt as though the whole forest stopped moving. Nobody made a sound.

Harker took Loria's place at the front of the group and she sprinted down the path to see where the guard was pointing.

She skidded to a halt at the side of the path, and sucked in a breath as she saw her across the valley. "KARA!" She screamed, waving her arms frantically.

"Not so loud." Draga moved towards her, watching the trees around us. Skygge stayed low, waiting at the back of the group beside me. His ears twitched occasionally as a bird flew above us, or a squirrel ran through the trees. I took a few steps forward, peering over the edge of the mountain to see Kara standing below us. She had a small girl beside her, clutching close to her body.

"She has Isha!" I whispered, turning to the girl's mother. Tears streamed down her face as she grasped my hands in her own.

"How will she reach us?" Harker called, pulling his cloak tighter around himself. The sun had suddenly disappeared, and a chill breeze was blowing through the trees.

"There's a path over there." Loria pointed a little way to our right.

She gestured wildly down to Kara, and after a few moments moved back to join the group. We set off towards a clearing where our path met the one Kara would climb. We hadn't made it far before a low rumble made me stop still. I looked around, trying to find the source of the sound, until I realised it was Skygge.

"What is it?" I whispered, crouching down to hold my face in front of his.

He wouldn't look at me, staring up at the snow covered mountains.

"Draga!" I called out, standing up warily. He was the closest guard. He made his way over, eyeing Skygge cautiously.

"What is it?" He glared at me. Skygge growled again, louder this time. I looked up, following Skygge's eyes to the mountain tops.

"Avalanche." Draga mumbled, storming off to the front of the group. "AVALANCHE!"

...

Panic crushed me like a wave. The clearing ahead sat sheltered by an overhanging cliff, but we'd never make it in time.

The children were screaming, grabbing any adult they could find and clinging to them desperately with their tiny frozen hands.

"Move!" Draga was shouting now, louder than before. He herded the villagers forwards, like cattle at a market.

The crowd of bodies moved like an ocean, moving past me in one huge mass. A few of the smaller children were moving too slowly, their little legs not fast enough to keep up with the rest. Loria lifted two of the children up, and I did the same, carrying them forward on our hips as we ran. I looked over my shoulder to see the guards doing the same, bringing up the rear. The children screamed, burying their faces in the folds of our cloaks. They had no idea what was going on.

The noise of the snow falling was deafening. It fell in huge powdery sheets, slamming into the path where we had been standing moments before. The last of us sprinting for the clearing were engulfed by the snow that hung in the air like a veil.

We spluttered as we reached the others, mothers grabbing their children as we tried to catch our breath.

Loria rubbed her face frantically, trying to free herself from the ice that coated it. She rushed over to the edge of the cliff, crying out to Kara. She turned to us then, watching as Harker counted heads to make sure every villager was accounted for. He nodded at Draga, and Loria tried to smile.

"We are safe, for now." Draga took up one of the leather bags that had been thrown under the trees, swinging it over his huge shoulders. The fallen snow was tumbling over the cliff like a frozen waterfall, piling up on the ground.

Chapter Nineteen

It felt as though the avalanche sent us back to square one. It took most of the afternoon to clear the fallen snow so we were able to wade through to the edge of the cliff. Loria sent a few of the stronger adults out to attempt a rescue. Kara was carrying Isha on her back, scaling the side of the mountain towards us. She'd finally found a safe path to the cliffs edge, and the rescuers began dropping ropes down to pull her up.

Isha's mother stood anxiously by the edge of the group, pacing and rubbing her frozen hands together. She was a tall woman, taller than most. Her hair was golden and fell in ringlets down her back.

Her dark skin gleamed in the last of the sunlight, and her eyes sparkled despite the worry they carried.

"Isha will be okay. Kara has been with her the whole time." I said, laying my hand gently on her shoulder. She was shaking.

"She is so small. She will be half frozen!" She frowned, hugging herself against the snow.

"Alura!"

I turned to find Kara climbing over the edge of the cliff, Isha strapped carefully to her back with strips of torn fabric, covered in fresh snow.

I rushed over to help pull her up, my hands numb but determined to drag my friend to safety. It wasn't long before Loria joined us. She threw her arms around Kara, tears welling in her eyes. Harker appeared from nowhere and untied Isha from Kara's back, carrying the girl over to her mother.

She was pale, and weak, and clung to Harker desperately. I wasn't sure she even knew who Harker was, but it didn't seem to matter to her. Draga wrapped a large woollen blanket around Kara's shoulders, and sat her down by a pile of dry sticks where a small boy was trying to create a flame. He clicked his fingers furiously, his brows furrowed and his eyes narrow. Finally a flame sprung up from his hand, and he buried it into the pile of wood.

Soon the fire was roaring, and Kara sat drinking in the warmth.

"How are you feeling?" I smiled, sitting down beside her.

"Better." She nodded, although she didn't look it.

...

That evening, I joined Kara and Loria by the fire, along with some of the older villagers. The smoke rose high above our heads, and tiny drops of rain fell around us as we huddled together to keep warm.We spent a long time discussing the Goddess with the elderly members of the group, their tales and stories were fascinating.

Soon the subject changed however, and I was learning much more about Eslanda and her reputation.

"There's others like us y'know." one elderly woman told me, "Dotted around the mountains, other side of the forest too."

"Except she got to those ones." A man grumbled, scratching his beard.

"What do you mean?" I frowned, turning to the old man.

"I'm not sure…" Loria began but the man interrupted her.

"She got 'em." He growled, staring into the fire. "Thinks it makes her stronger or somethin', that's what I heard."

"How many?" I whispered, horrified.

"All together? Few hundred they say, could be thousands." the man tutted, shaking his head.

"Why? I thought she was angry at your village?"

"She was, but the more villages came to our aid, the more people got in her way." The old woman explained.

We set off up the mountain as soon as the sun rose above the horizon. It was bitterly cold, but we wrapped ourselves in our thickest cloaks and trudged through the snow.

 Skygge stalked along beside me, his ears twitching at every sound. It was still snowing, but it fell much lighter and didn't stick to our cloaks as we stumbled up the hills.

Kara walked alone at the front of the group, staring silently ahead through the mist.

"I think she saw something." Loria whispered, pulling her cloak up around her face and moving to walk closer by my side.

"Saw what?" I kept my eyes forward, something told me we shouldn't be discussing Kara like this.

"Something bad. She's even quieter than usual. I mean, I know she's tired and she's been through enough just trying to get back to us..." Loria chewed her lip anxiously.

"But I think there's something else."

"If she saw something we needed to know about, she'd tell us." I nodded, more to reassure myself than anything else. Loria tried to smile, but her eyes told me she wasn't so sure.

Kara was always confident, and the sudden change in her personality was a shock.

She was lacking the usual confidence that came so naturally to her, and her orders were almost always followed by a questioning glance over at Loria. I could tell that Loria was struggling with it too. She relied on Kara to make the decisions and lead the group, and she was clearly worried about her friend.

I tried to take some of the pressure from them both, keeping the younger villagers entertained at the back of the group, encouraging them through the hours and hours of hiking.

Some of the children were struggling now, dragging their feet and shivering uncontrollably. Loria and I took turns carrying them alongside the parents, wrapping them in our cloaks to let them rest and stay warm for a while. Isha's mother stayed close to us, ever thankful for her daughter's safe return. Isha was quiet, although not so much as Kara. She didn't say much about what happened, and she wouldn't make eye contact when anyone asked her about it.

Chapter Twenty

I woke suddenly to the sound of heavy breathing. Gasping, I dragged myself up onto my elbows in the dark. Something wet rubbed against my cheek and I shrugged away. I held out my hand and felt the familiar soft feeling of Skygge's fur beneath my fingers. I let out a sigh and sat up, scratching his ears.

"You woke me up..." I yawned, trying to force my eyes to adjust to the darkness. "What's going on?"

Skygge nudged my shoulder with his nose again as if to force me up.

I unravelled myself from the blankets and wrapped myself in my cloak. He was staring at me intently, and nudged me forward towards the edge of the forest.

"What are you showing me?" I whispered, reaching out ahead of me to feel my way through the trees. An old branch lay fallen on the ground, and I stumbled as I tried to climb over it.

Skygge ran ahead slightly, snorting lightly in the cold air.

I struggled through the trees and snaking roots until I bumped into Skygge where he sat patiently under a giant pine. His ears stood up, and he was studying something in the darkness.

"What is it?" I whispered, crouching down to his level. My eyes ached as I strained to see what he was seeing.

Skygge became restless, pacing and huffing. He nudged my hand and pushed it towards the base of the tree.

My hand met something small and soft, and I drew in a breath.

Fumbling in the dark, I gingerly picked up the tiny ball, bringing it up to my chest and wrapping it in my cloak.

Skygge nudged my leg gently and bounded off ahead. I made my way back to the camp slowly, feeling the small bundle in my cloak wriggle and squark. When I reached the campfire, I sat on one of the logs and carefully took the tiny creature from my cloak. The firelight sparkled as I peered down at the tiny crow in my lap. It's wing was bent at an alarming angle, and I muttered under my breath as it struggled to move around.

"What's going on?" came a voice behind me, and Kara appeared through the darkness. I looked at her in surprise, and she shrugged. "I couldn't sleep."

"He's injured." I nodded at the tiny crow struggling in my hands as I tried to calm the frightened creature.

"Is it wild?" She asked, sitting beside me on the old log by the fire.

"Yes. It must have fallen from it's nest." I sighed, looking around in the darkness.

"There's a healer here, isn't there?" I asked, looking up at Kara's pale face. The fire cast strange shadows across her cheeks and she seemed much older than I knew she was.

Kara nodded, pushing her hair away from her face.

"She's been with us for a long time. What do you need?"

I looked the bird over carefully, and wrapped it back up in my cloak.

"It needs moonbalm." I told her, standing up and offering a hand. "I don't wish to wake her, but the wing is broken." I gestured to the bird bundled in my cloak and Kara nodded.

"This way."

Chapter Twenty-One

"Shari?" Kara shook the young girl sleeping by the edge of the camp. She sat up sleepily, rubbing her eyes and blinking at us.

"Kara? Is that you?" she asked, squinting at us in the moonlight.

"Yes, we need your help Shari..." she nodded, wrapping the young girl in the cloak laying by her belongings on the floor.

"I'm sorry to wake you Shari." I told her, "I've been told you're a gifted healer, and I need your help to save this little one..." I smiled, showing her the tiny crow.

Her face lit up, and she nodded eagerly.

"Do you have any moonbalm?" I asked, and she scrunched up her face in thought. It was the only healing leaf I knew of, and they had used it on one of the young girls after the last ceremony. Turning to a huge woven bag laying on the wet grass, she dug through its contents and pulled out a small glass jar.

"Here!" she nodded, handing it to me. The leaves glistened with a layer of opal-like crystals.

"Yes, do you think it will work?" I asked, taking her hand to help her across the pitch-black camp. We settled by the fire and Shari opened the jar, pulling out one of the leaves.

"It is good for breaks. I will do what I can." she looked at the bird.

I nodded, "Can you prepare it for me now?"

I knew very little of magical healing, and it fascinated me to watch the little girl work. She popped one of the moonleaves into her mouth and chewed it a few times, then reached out to take the tiny bird into her lap.

It wriggled and flapped, trying to break free and Shari frowned.

"Can you make it keep still?" she asked, her brows furrowed in frustration. I reached out and placed a hand on the birds wing, feeling a warmth move through me into the tiny creature.

"Thank you." Shari smiled, looking over at me in awe as the tiny creature lay still, content and sleeping. She pulled the leaf from her lips, and pressed it into the break in the bird's wing.

Chapter Twenty-Two

There was an uneasy feeling surrounding the camp the next day, although everyone did their best to shake it off. Children sat playing in the grass by the fire, where the ice had melted and the dew was slowly drying. The twins I'd met before sat arguing about something, and a group of girls made chains with flowers that Kara had grown for them earlier that morning. "Kara was asking for you." Harker called from beside the fire. He was drinking from a large copper cup, his breath fogging the cold air. I nodded, walking past him towards the only real tent in the camp. If she was anywhere, it would be there.

"We're all to meet her there at midday." He nodded, staring at me as I continued on my way. The tent was dark, but much warmer than the chill air outside. I pushed through the rough fabric door, and Loria sat on a large woolen blanket on the floor with Kara stood opposite her, brushing her long white hair with her fingers and tying it up loosely.

"Alura." Kara tuned as I entered, wrapping her thin arms around me and folding me into a hug. "Are you well?"

"Very." I assured her, sitting beside Loria on the blanket and looking up at Kara in anticipation.

"Alura, I realise you've been thrown into our world too quickly.

Nobody has even explained to you about harnessing your gifts, have they?" Kara asked, sitting opposite us on the floor, her long legs tucked elegantly beneath her. I shook my head, unsure where this was going.

"It's important that you learn." She smiled, "You're a great asset to us Alura. Only you can do what you do."

I bit my lip anxiously, the tent feeling hotter by the second.

"You need me to do something?" I asked, and Loria put her hand on my shoulder.

"Eslanda is coming for us Alura." She sighed, pulling her knees up under her chin and hugging her legs close to her.

"Have you seen her?" I frowned, looking to Kara for answers.

She shook her head and her hair fell loose, tumbling over her shoulders. Sighing, she pulled it back and tied it again, rubbing her temples.

"One of the children." She gestured outside the tent. "He has... visions."

"Some say he sees the future." Loria told me, "but really he can see what is happening elsewhere in the world."

"And he saw Eslanda?" I looked from Loria to Kara, a chill running down my spine.

"He said she is close." Kara nodded, rubbing her temples. Her eyes were dark and the skin beneath them was a deep blue.

"We've got this far." I said, trying to sound reassuring.

"You don't understand." Kara frowned.

She tried to smile as she pushed a stray curl from my face. "She has wild creatures with her. The young boy said it was like an army."

...

Kara held a meeting at midday, and we all crammed into the only real tent we had. Loria sat beside me, with Harker and Draga. A few of the stronger men she'd set as guards joined us, and Shari sat by the fire, the only true healer we had. She explained the situation, and brought in the young boy who told us of the vision he'd had of Eslanda and her army of wild creatures. After the meeting had ended, Kara dismissed everyone except for Loria and I, and we sat in the tent silently for a long time. Skygge lay curled up beside me, so calm and still it seemed he was frozen in time. Our bond was so strong at this point, that we seemed almost as one.

Kara and Loria seemed to barely notice his presence, and the villagers no longer shrunk away from him.

"Loria, I need you to take Alura to the forest. Just to the edge, don't go too far. Take her there and keep her safe." Kara said suddenly, her voice thick with concentration and uncertainty. "You need to harness your gift." She looked up at me, and I stood up immediately.

If truth be told, I had been desperate to try and connect with the wild creatures. I'd done it before, and it had happened so naturally that I was eager to try it again.

"Take your time." Loria told me, as we made our way across the camp to the edge of the forest. The trees were darker on the west side of the camp, so we made for the east side, where the sun was peeking through the leaves. I sat on the ground by the trunk of a huge pine. It's roots twisted in the earth beneath me and I buried my hands in the dirt. I could feel the life around me. I sat beneath the tree for a long time, silent and waiting.

 Skygge lay beside me, his ears flat against his head, relaxed and calm. The wind was picking up, and leaves whirled around us, making it hard to see. Loria stood silently on the edge of the forest, protected by the overhanging trees and watching me intently. A sudden warmth hit me, and Skygge sat up, his ears twitching as he scanned the area anxiously. Closing my eyes, I held out my hands, trying to remember the ritual I had performed so long ago. The wind subsided, the leaves fell gracefully to the ground, and I felt gentle breathing on my upturned palms.

Opening my eyes slowly, my heart began pounding in my chest. An pack of wolves and wild dogs sat calmly in the clearing in front of me.

The branches above me were bustling with energy, and there were hundreds of tiny birds perched on them, staring down at me.

Slowly, I got to my feet and took a few steps towards the largest wolf of the pack. Skygge moved quickly to stand beside me, his fur bristling.

I held out my hand, and waited.

I could feel Loria's eyes on me, watching to see if I was ready. The wolf tipped it's huge grey head down, and nuzzled my hand, before turning back to it's pack. It howled, the sound echoing through the forest. The rest of the pack joined in, before disappearing back into the trees.

Turning back towards the edge of the forest, I caught a glimpse of Loria smiling from the corner of my eye, and allowed myself a moment of pride.

I am ready.

Chapter Twenty-Three

Word spread quickly through the camp, and it
wasn't long before the villagers were hounding
Kara for information.

"An army? Are the regular folk after us?" one
man demanded, squaring up to Kara as best he
could. Draga forced his way in front of her, and
Harker stood close by.

"Are they coming to kill us?" another man
pushed in, the crowd growing outside Kara's
tent.

"Nobody is coming to kill us." Kara shook her
head, clearly frustrated with the entire
situation.

"There's been talk of an army though. Who's coming?" the first man crossed his heavy arms and leaned against a tree.

His face was hard and cold, and he glared at Kara suspiciously.

"Nobody is coming for us." Kara repeated, holding her head up and staring the man down.

"You best be telling us the truth girl." the man scowled.

"None of us asked for you to be in charge of this. You best not be lying." He stomped off towards the other side of the camp, and Kara sighed heavily. The crowd gradually dispersed, and everyone went back to whatever they had been doing before Kara had been ambushed.

"Are you alright?" I asked, grabbing her wrist as she made for the tent again.

She nodded unconvincingly and gestured for me to follow her.

"I knew their suspicions would grow." Kara huffed, dropping to the floor and bringing her knees up under her chin. She was so used to leading our unruly group of villagers by now, that I often forgot how young she was.

She seemed so much older than her age, and it was only in times like this that I remembered the truth.

"I shouldn't lie to them. They've been suspicious of me and my plans since we left the Forge." she said, looking to Loria desperately.

"Well, all they knew was that we were making for the Forge... So of course they were suspicious when we continued on." Loria nodded. "But we can't just tell them about Eslanda."

"They know about her!" Kara shook her head angrily.

"Word spreads like wildfire. Someone was probably eavesdropping on our meeting."

I watched the two argue for a while, and buried my shaking hands in Skygge's fur. He always gave me a deep feeling of safety. Kara stood up to take a copper cup from the small wooden table in the centre of the tent, but it crashed to the ground as screams echoed through the camp.

Panic washed over us as we scrambled out of the tent, Skygge busting into the cool air first, us following closely. I heard Skygge's growls before I realised what was happening. The villagers had descended into chaos. People were fighting and scrabbling to get away into the forest.

The screams and shouting voices made it hard to think clearly, but eventually my mind settled onto the scene that lay before me.

Blood covered the wet grass in the centre of camp and the fire was burning out, sending smoke into the air in huge clouds.

Coughing, and trying to fight our way through the smoke and panicked bodies, I stumbled to a halt as I made out the shapes of wolves and wild dogs in the distance, howling and running towards us.

"What's happening?" Loria screamed over the shouting and howling, and I shook my head in despair. There were children crying and fighting their way to safety, hiding under trees and huge fallen branches. Two of the wolves circled us as we fought to drag the remaining villagers out of camp and into the forest, hoping it was the right thing to do. If these creatures attacking us were wild, who knew where was safe?

"Alura!" Kara grabbed me by the shoulders and stared at me desperately. There was blood on her face, and her white hair was smeared red and brown.

"I need you to fight them." Fight them. The words echoed in my mind as I twisted round to find the entire wolf pack standing before me. "Skygge." I whispered, and felt the warmth of his soft fur.

Not taking my eyes from the wolf pack, I motioned towards the villagers hiding in the forest. "Shadow, take Kara." I told him, and he growled. "Now." I hissed, and he slunk off into the trees with Kara following close behind. These wolves, they were the same pack from the forest. The ones I had seen with Loria.

From the corner of my eye I spotted her watching me, full of disbelief. She knew.

The wolves were still circling me, their golden eyes following my every move. I watched them close in on me, their growls penetrating my skull until I could hear them vibrating inside my own head.

I could feel their heartbeats, feel their breathing on my skin.

"You do not belong here!" I shouted, and they stopped, confused and unsure.The leader of the pack lowered it's head, growling at my and stalking forward inch by inch.

"You do not belong here!" I screamed this time, and the wolf jumped back, as if in pain rather than shock. It yelped and retreated a few paces.

"I know what you are." I whispered, moving towards the pack with slow but determined steps. "You are not alone."

Chapter Twenty-Four

The camp's mood changed from panic to despair as I helped Shari attend the wounded. It turned out that the wolves were not the only wild creatures attacking. Smaller creatures had caught the children while they were playing. Snakes, spiders, scorpions.

"You scared the wolves away..." a voice whispered as I pulled moonleaves from Shari's jars and handed them to her.

I looked up to find a small boy staring back at me, his dark grey eyes wide with wonder. I didn't know what to say to him.

"I don't think I scared them. I just told them to go away." I smiled, ruffling the boys hair.

"Is it sore?" Shari asked, motioning towards the bite on a young boy's leg. He shook his head, dark curls swinging gently around his round face.

"Good." Shari grinned, standing up. "If it starts to hurt again, you must come and find me. Do you understand?"

The boy nodded and ran back to his mother, who was waiting nearby with a group of women and children by the fire.

"She's clever." I whispered as Shari looked around the camp for the next villager to attend to.

"Who?" Shari frowned, rummaging in her bag for more linen bandages.

"Eslanda."

"You mean, you think she sent them?" she asked, wide eyed.

"She was using them. Controlling them." I said, handing her the linen bandages I had prepared. She took them, shaking her head.

"Can you do that?" She looked up at me, then away at the villagers dotted around camp.

"No." I told her, and she didn't say anything else.

It took us most of three hours to tend to the rest of the injured folk. Most of the children didn't seem to mind, it was as if they hadn't felt their injuries at all.

Once the last villager had been treated, I returned the jars to Shari and headed off to the forest.

Skygge stalked beside me, scanning our surroundings constantly.

"You tell me if you see anything." I told him, and he ran ahead of me into the trees. I found a small clearing not far from the edge of camp, and sat against the trunk of an old pine tree. It was damp from recent rains, and not the most comfortable place but I tried to ignore that. Burying my hands in the dirt, I closed my eyes and breathed in the smoky air.

I thought about the Goddess, after all, she was the one who gave me this gift. Maybe she could teach me how to use it.

I sat for a long while, pleading with her silently and listening to Skygge's gentle breaths as he lay beside me on the grass.

"You know what to do Alura."

My eyes flew open and I sat up, my breath stuck in my throat.

"You are stronger than you believe."

It took a while, but my eyes finally focused on the trees ahead of me, and I could make out a figure coming towards me.

"Goddess of Light…" I whispered with disbelief as the figure settled in front of me, reaching out to Skygge. He sat up, lowering his head to let the Goddess stroke him comfortingly.

"I don't want to fight them." I said after a few moments of silence.

My heart was pounding in my chest, my hands were sweaty and I felt lightheaded, but I tried to stay focused on what I was seeing.

"You will not fight them." she smiled, holding out her hand. I took it nervously in my own, and felt the warmth of her magic flowing through me. "You will be one with them."

"But, what about Eslanda?" I asked, pulling myself up to stand opposite the Goddess in her pool of glowing light. Warmth radiated from her.

"You will not fight her." the Goddess told me, her fiery eyes consuming me.

"We have to fight her, she'll attack us again, but I don't think she'll use the wild creatures this time." I said, tears running down my frozen face.

I hadn't realised how scared I truly was.

"She will attack." the Goddess agreed, "But you will not fight her."

I was starting to regret asking her for her guidance, as she was confusing me more than she was answering my questions. She seemed to sense my emotions and pulled me into her arms. Heat overcame me and I felt myself glow with her power and strength.

"Be strong Alura." she whispered, "She will not break you."

Chapter Twenty-Five

I don't remember falling asleep, but I was woken by Kara shaking me violently.

"Alura!" she pulled me to my feet, peering into my eyes, her face concerned and panicked. "We couldn't find you!" Loria grabbed me, pulling me into a hug and demanding an explanation. Skygge barked at the girls until they fussed over him, then he sunk down onto the ground and watched me carefully. I started to explain, and Kara interrupted me.

"We'll go back to camp and talk... Loria will take you to the tent while I find Harker and let him know you're safe.

We sent him into the forest on the other side of camp to search for you."

Suddenly I felt guilty, but Kara had turned and headed off before I could apologise. Loria took my arm and led me back across the forest. We made it to the tent before Kara had returned, and Loria told me to sit by the table, handing me a cup and sitting down opposite me.

"You're warm." she frowned, obviously concerned.

"I'm fine." I smiled reassuringly, just as Kara came through the door of the tent.

"Alright, tell us what happened." She said, settling onto the ground between Loria and I. Sighing, I tried my best to explain to them what I had experienced.

"You saw her?" Loria asked, her mahogany eyes wide and sparkling.

"She came to me when I called for her. She said we will not be defeated." I told them, and Kara chewed her lip.

"We should still prepare." she nodded, although she seemed to be discussing the situation with herself more than with us.

"I feel stronger." I whispered, stroking Skygge as he lay his head in my lap and stared up at me.

"She has blessed you." Loria told me. "She knows we need you more than anything else right now." I wasn't sure what she meant, but it made me feel better.

"Kara?" Harker called from outside the tent. His head appeared through the door and Kara waved him in.

"Do we have a plan?" Kara shifted uncomfortably, but nodded.

She was still chewing her lip nervously, and her hair was still stained with blood.

"Also," Harker added, moving to sit beside her on the ground. "Draga has been acting... strangely." he frowned.

"How so?" Loria demanded. It was obvious that Loria was not so keen on Draga as Kara was. He was strong, and stubborn, and he was a good guard, but Loria and I had both become suspicious of him.

"He's quiet, not so argumentative. He doesn't talk to me, or the other guards." Harker explained. "He disappears at night sometimes too."

"Why are you only now telling me this?" Kara snapped, her eyes angry and dark. "How long has this been going on?" Harker looked hurt, but he continued all the same.

"Since we left the Forge."

"Do you think he is dangerous?" Loria asked, sensing the tension growing. "Do you think he's..."

Harker cut her off before she could finish her question. "Perhaps." he nodded.

"We need a plan. A new plan." Kara announced, standing up and taking her old leather bag from the table.

"Harker, leave us." she said, without looking at him. He started to object, but she shot him a look that told him not to argue.

Silently, he left the tent and I heard his footsteps crunch against the fallen leaves and pine needles covering the grass outside.

"We need to move on." Kara sighed, pulling a map from her bag. She laid it out across the blanket between us, and traced the river with a pale finger.

"Where will we go?" Loria whispered, looking down at the old map.

"Farther North." was the only destination Kara gave us, and we took that as all we would get.

"We'll leave in the morning. You two sleep in here tonight, I will set guards outside."

Chapter Twenty-Six

As soon as the sun appeared over the trees,
Kara woke us and told us to get ready to leave.
Harker was helping the villagers prepare when
I stumbled out into the morning and found
Shari picking weeds and herbs from the
clearing by the camp.

"I want to be prepared." she mumbled when
she saw me watching her.

"I can help. What do you need?" I crouched
beside her and she handed me a jar.

The label read lightweed. I'd seen it before, but
a long time ago.

I set to digging through weeds and bushes trying to find some lightweed leaves, when I found a bunch of plants growing together.

I plucked off a few leaves, thanked the Goddess for letting me take them, and placed them carefully in the jar. I handed the jar back to Shari, and helped her pack her bag with the many other bottles and pouches she had collected.

The camp was alive with movement and energy. It seemed as if everyone was happy just to be on the move again. I helped a few villagers pack bags, and fastened cloaks onto the younger children.

Some followed Skygge around the camp, chasing him and stroking his soft, dense fur. "They don't see many tame ones." an elderly woman smiled from under the hood of a very oversized cloak.

I smiled. "I'm glad they have the chance now." It took a while to get everyone moving, but eventually we headed farther through into forest. Kara and Loria led the group, followed by Harker and I.

Draga stayed close behind, but Kara had placed guards at the back of the group, as well as either side and at the front, between us. After what Harker had told her, she wasn't taking any chances. Skygge walked calmly beside me, taking in our surroundings and scanning constantly for any sign of a threat.

"We walk until nightfall." Kara told us as we reached a small stream.

She stopped to fill bottles with water, and a few of the villagers waded in to cool down. The air was crisp and cold, but there was no rain, and the walking was hard work, so I didn't blame them.

The wind was starting to pick up, and I hugged my cloak tighter around myself as we set off again and left the little stream behind. Isha had taken to walking at the front of the group with us, and it was nice seeing her so much more talkative. She walked close to Skygge, and talked to him as we walked along a tiny stone path through the woods.

"Does he talk to you?" Isha asked suddenly, taking me by surprise.

"Kind of." I laughed, patting his head as he walked beside us protectively.

"But not with words."

Isha screwed her face up at me. "How can he talk to you without words?" she asked, confused and more than a little sceptical.

"Well, he tells me things with his mind." I tried to explain it to her, but the harder I tried the more complicated it got.

"That sounds weird." Isha decided, shaking her head. She carried on walking in silence then, only occasionally talking to Skygge.

We reached a ridge, and found that we were actually on the edge of a cliff. The mountain's edge fell away at our feet and I grabbed onto Skygge to keep my balance. The world seemed to spin around me as I peered over the edge into the gaping hole below us.

Kara came up beside me, and took my arm gently but forcefully.

"You see that waterfall over there?" she asked, pointing across the huge chasm between us and the other mountains.

I nodded, leaning away from the cliff's edge.

"That's where we'll head. We can follow the path, then make our way down." she explained, squeezing my arm reassuringly.

"Kara, quiet!" Harker hissed, pulling us back from the edge of the cliff.

"What?" Kara glared at him, and he put his finger to his lips.

One of the guards Kara had set at the front of the group repeated the motion, and signalled towards the other end of the path we'd been following.

"Someone is following us." the guard nodded, and Harker drew a knife from his side. The two of them walked slowly but purposefully towards the end of the path, and disappeared behind a thick line of trees. I looked from Kara to Loria desperately, and tried to calm my breathing. Has she been following us? Shouting echoed through the trees and branches cracked under running feet. Harker burst through the trees first, followed by the guard, who was restraining a tall woman with tumbling red hair.

Her eyes were the deepest shade of red, and seemed to glow.

I was about to let out a gasp when a hand clamped over my mouth and I was dragged backwards. Panicking, I kicked out and swung my arms frantically, catching Loria as I squirmed to get free. She turned, her black hair fanning around her head as she spotted me in the distance.

"Alura!" she screamed, launching into a sprint as she chased after me. Her screams caught the attention of the rest of the group, and even Harker turned his attention from the guard and their captive. A huge guard stepped out from between two giant oaks, and aimed an arrow straight at the person holding me. My breathing was rapid, and my heart was beating so hard I feared it would burst through my skin.

"Draga. Let her go." Harker growled, appearing beside the guard with the bow.

His arrow was still aimed just above my head. Draga's grumbling voice rattled my mind as he tightened his grip on me, his hands hot and sweaty.

"You won't beat Eslanda without her." Draga smirked, and Harker fumbled with his knife. They're all counting on me. I'm their only hope. I tried to speak, but Draga only squeezed tighter, muffling my voice.

"Have you been planning this?" Harker asked, although even I knew that was a stupid question. I could hear the hurt in his voice. My mind flashed back to when I'd first arrived at Willow Hall. Draga had taken an instant dislike to me, and he'd not been too shy to show it either. We should have known.

"Let her go." Harker repeated, his voice breaking slightly. I didn't know if he was scared to lose me, or his only chance at beating Eslanda.

Either way, he was trying to protect me, and that was good enough. Draga moved to drag me further from the group, but something flew past my ear and made a wet thud. Draga's hand fell from my mouth and I rushed forward, grabbing Harker. He pushed me behind him, but didn't take his eyes from Draga.

I didn't want to look, but I knew I had to. Draga lay bleeding on the mossy ground, his eyes vacant and unmoving. I shuddered.

In unison, Harker and I turned and found Kara standing on a dead tree trunk, a bow in her hand.

She nodded, grimacing at the body of her former friend lying on the ground. Before I had time to thank her, the guard holding the woman from the woods cried out, and we stumbled back through the trees to find him bleeding from one arm, and holding the Eslanda with the other.

Her face was as pale as fresh snow, and her hair was made of flames. It would have curled in gentle ringlets down to her waist, but the guard was holding it roughly to stop her running away. I didn't have to be told who she was. I moved towards her, my heart thudding but my head held high.

"You will not fight her." the Goddess' voice echoed in my mind, and I stopped mid-stride. Staring at her, she smirked at me. Just then, howling filled the air and I turned to find Skygge barking frantically.

In every gap between every tree, there stood one of her wild creatures. My heart sank. Loria stepped beside me and took my hand in hers. "You won't fight this alone." she whispered, and I squeezed her hand in response. The wild creatures closed in on us, the whole group trapped. There were wolves, foxes, bears, dogs, stags, and all of them had piercing red eyes. Red, like Eslanda.

Chapter Twenty-Seven

Loria was shaking beside me, her hands as cold as ice. The children were being herded away from the wild creatures, but they still cried out in fear. Panic hit me like a lightning bolt, and I felt my heart thudding so hard I could hear it as clearly as the thunder crashing above our heads.

You don't have a choice in this Alura. Look at them!

I made myself breathe, and look at the terrified faces of the villagers huddling together in a mass of shaking bodies. *They'll all die if you don't stop this.*

My legs felt heavy and I fell to the ground,
pushing myself up with my shaking arms.
Loria made to grab for me but I shook her off.
"You're stronger than you know" the Goddess
whispered, and a heat like fire itself hit me, so
real that it pushed me down to the ground.
"Get up. Get up, get up, get up." I hissed,
pushing myself onto my knees, then back up
onto my feet.

 It was then that I realised something. Skygge
hadn't moved. I'd fallen to the ground, been
overcome with an immense heat and he'd not
so much as twitched his ear. A new fear shot
through me, and I looked from the red-eyed
wild creatures, to my own Skygge. I held my
hand out to him, and he nudged it gently with
his wet nose. He's still mine.

The wild creatures were still circling us,
crushing us closer and closer together. Get up.
Forcing myself forward, I stumbled away from
the group, and knelt down before the largest of
the wild creatures. The same wolf I'd met many
times now. In that moment I knew, this wolf is

not just any a wolf after all... it was a dog, and it was Eslanda's companion.

I felt her tense, and saw from the corner of my eye her knuckles turn white as she clenched her hands into fists. I reached out and placed my hand on the dog's head, feeling that same intense heat as before, but this time it passed through me. It ran down my arm and through my fingers, like it was as much a part of me as my own blood.

"Don't touch him!" Eslanda cried out, and my head snapped towards her. I was breaking her. I watched in shock as the dog's eyes flickered shut, then opened wide, a gold so bright it shone.

Eslanda lashed out and fought free from the guard holding her by the edge of the circle. She screamed, running towards me with her flaming red hair flowing wildly behind her. Just as she reached me, a familiar whizzing sound burst through the air, and Eslanda went down with a thud. As she fell, she caught my arm and I felt a burning sensation as if I'd been scolded.

As Kara dragged Eslanda away from me, I ran my hand over the burn on my arm, wincing. The wild creatures were still circling us, their heads low to the ground and their red eyes threatening.

A huge brown bear lunged at the villagers, sending the whole group into chaos.

I pushed the pain in my arm from my mind and waded through the people to reach the bear, standing tall on its hind legs.

"Stop!" I screamed, anger and frustration taking over.

"Stop it!" The bear stopped, looking at me puzzled, as if it understood me, but was shocked at what I was saying.

"You are not hers!" I shouted, pointing at Eslanda, bleeding from her leg where an arrow had pierced her icy white skin. The bear growled, and lunged at me, but as its huge paw connected with my body, I felt fire flood through me. The bear yelped, darting away as if it had run straight into wildfire.

 I held up my hands to inspect them, astonished to find heat waves surrounding them. I was on fire.

I knelt down, burying my hands into the dirt and forced the fire out, watching as a ring of flames surrounded us. Looking up, I stepped through it, untouched.

I could still hear the villagers screaming, and Skygge was barking frantically as he saw me disappear through the wall of fire.

"Alura!" Loria cried, and I felt her fear. I walked through the circle, holding my hand out and touching each of the wild creatures as I passed them.

I turned to find the army of wild creatures standing before me, their eyes studying me closely. Eslanda struggled to stand up, and came towards me again, blood trickling down her leg. Kara moved to grab her, but I raised my hand.

She hesitated, but let Eslanda pass. I stood, staring at her fiercely, and waited for her to reach me. My arm throbbed where she had burned me, but I tried to ignore it.

"They are not yours anymore Eslanda." I called, and she forced herself to walk harder and faster. A few times her bleeding leg buckled beneath her, but she was stronger than even I had expected. "They're wild. You cannot control them."

Chapter Twenty-Eight

The thunder was growing louder by the
minute, and lightning cracked across the sky,
illuminating us momentarily. It had grown
dark but I had hardly noticed, and now I had to
squint to make out Eslanda in the darkness.
She came at me with her hands curled into
fists, her hair swirling wildly around her in the
wind. Skygge stalked out of the trees and stood
his ground, growling defiantly.
Her own companion stood beside her, ears flat
against its head, eyes dark and threatening.

He wasn't under her control anymore, but that certainly didn't mean he was under mine. She moved towards Skygge and I stepped forward protectively.

"Touch him, and you will regret it." I hissed, a sudden anger taking over. My hands became red and started to smoke. Eslanda turned, taking me by surprise. She moved towards the group of villagers huddled together, and crouched beside her companion. It was only then that it struck me how huge the dog truly was. Its head was at least three times the size of Skygge's, and it's legs were powerful and strong.

She whispered something, and held her hands out towards the villagers. The dog howled, and ran towards the group, barking and snapping it's huge jaws.

The villagers panicked and Eslanda dived for Kara, who was watching the ensuing madness in amazement.

She screamed out in anger, and her elbow connected with Eslanda's jaw. Eslanda's legs kicked wildly, and knocked Kara to the ground, but she thrashed out and grabbed for her bow. Tears welled in Kara's eyes as she brought the arrow up to Eslanda's heart. Everything slowed down, and seemed to stop as we all turned to watch. The villagers stopped screaming, the wild creatures crowded in and Skygge stalked close to me, staring at them.

"I can't let you do this." Kara growled, tears streaming down her face.

"You abandoned me. This is what you deserve." Eslanda spat. The wild creatures were trapping the villagers, and some had already attacked. I heard cries and the unbearable snapping of bone as a huge grey wolf latched onto one of the guards. Then the others joined in, and the screaming started up again.

It got fainter and fainter as people were dragged away into the trees.

...

"They're innocent!" Kara sobbed over the screaming villagers. Eslanda ran towards her, slashing at her furiously.Kara grabbed her and slammed her to the floor, staring as she choked beneath her. "Make them stop!"

Eslanda smirked. "What if I don't?"

"Do it! Call them off, make them stop! Too many people have died Eslanda, too many innocent people.

We never abandoned you, you abandoned yourself, you abandoned the Goddess. You abandoned us." Kara shook her, a tiny line of blood running down Eslanda's shoulder where her nails had pierced the skin.

She struggled to sit up, her face so close to Kara's that their breath mingled in the cold air. She looked over at the wild creatures dragging the villagers away, the ground wet with rain and blood. Her eyes glittered, and she turned back to Kara and smiled.

"No."

...

Eslanda gasped, shuddering. Loria fell to her knees, tears streaming down her face. Kara screamed, falling onto Eslanda as Harker dropped his bow. It fell to the ground and he stepped forward. It took a moment for my mind to understand what was happening. "This has to stop." Kara sobbed, holding Eslanda's body and crying desperately. Harker put a shaking hand on her shoulder, "It had to stop."

Chapter Twenty-Nine

Midnight was a lonely time, darkness
smothering us in its heavy arms. We spent a
good many weeks wandering lost in the forest,
trying desperately to find a way home. The
shadows came alive at night, tricking us, and
leading us in circles through the maze of trees.
"My father taught me to study the stars." Kara
told me one night, as we wrapped ourselves in
blankets by the fire.
The villagers huddled close together for
warmth, and we built as many fires as we
dared.

"Can you read them to find a way out?" I asked, staring up at the onyx sky, tiny diamonds dotted across the darkness above our heads.

"Maybe." She nodded, tugging at her blanket and hugging herself against the cold. It had been snowing for days, but for now it had settled down, and we stopped to enjoy the clearness of the sky.

It had been hard telling Kara and Loria that I was planning to return home. They had wanted me to join them at the Forge, to help rebuild Willow Hall.

"I have a family waiting for me." I frowned, shaking my head. "They have no idea where I've been, or what happened to me since I left."

"You're right, you should return to them." Loria nodded, putting an arm round my shoulders. "You will visit us though, won't you?"

"As soon as I can, I will help rebuild the Hall. You will need all the help you can get." I promised, which seemed to bring them some comfort.

The sun had set and we were toasting berries on the fire, while Kara studied the stars and made notes in a tiny leather book she'd had tucked in her bag.

"I think I've got it!" she said suddenly, sitting up and pointing through the forest. "If we follow that star, the one between those two peaks-" she gestured desperately, trying to make sure we knew what she was showing us. "if we follow that, we should make it back to the path! Back down the little mountain, over the hill and back towards the Forge!"

Loria beamed, squeezing her friend's arm excitedly. "I knew you'd figure it out!"

"We'll sleep here tonight, build up our strength and move on tomorrow. Midday should give us time to pack up and eat." Kara nodded, looking round at the villagers sleeping beside small fires. There were only thirty-two survivors, and it weighed heavily on Kara. She had barely mentioned Eslanda, and went quiet as she watched the villagers following us silently through the trees.

Midday brought warmth and the first clear sky in days. The sun cast flickering shadows on the slowly drying earth, and the children ran through the snow, laughing. Once everyone was standing together with bags slung over their shoulders, we headed through the woods towards the point on the horizon that Kara had mentioned the night before.

Harker carried one of the weaker children, a small boy with severe bite wounds.

He was smiling, jesting with his friends, but his wound was swollen and healing slowly. Loria and I took turns carrying some of the younger children, who struggled walking so far in one go without resting. They held on tightly, burying their faces in our cloaks and snoring softly. The streams were overflowing with the recent snowfall, and we had to walk wide of them to avoid the swollen banks. It took almost until sundown but when we finally found the path down the mountain a wave of relief rushed over me. The edge of the mountain fell away gradually, a rough path etched in the rock.

We attached the ropes to the largest trees across the ledge, and one by one climbed down to the bottom. Two of the guards led the group, waiting at the bottom to help us down. A few times the rock came away under my fingertips and I swung away from the mountainside, but I kept my balance and waited with the group for the next climber to descend.

We decided to lower Skygge down second to last, and Kara lifted him gently over the edge. As she gradually let the rope go over the cliff, Skygge hung suspended in the cool air as he made his way down slowly. I sent the rope back up to Kara, and watched nervously as she tied it tightly around her waist. Her white hair caught the last of the sun, shining silver as it swirled around her head in the wind. She hopped onto the ground, coiled up the rope and tucked it over her shoulder.

We stopped at the lake to collect more water, filling cups and bottles. The sun had disappeared behind the trees, and we started a fire to rest for the night. Tomorrow was the final push, if we started early we could make it to the Forge.

Harker carried one of the weaker children, a small boy with bite wounds.

He was smiling, jesting with his friends, but his wound was swollen and healing slowly.

Kara, Loria and I took turns carrying some of the younger children, the ones who struggled walking so far in one go without resting.

They held on tightly, burying their faces in our cloaks and snoring softly.

The streams were overflowing with the recent snowfall, and we had to walk wide of them to avoid the swollen banks. It took almost until sundown but when we finally found the path down the mountain a wave of relief rushed over me. The edge of the mountain fell away gradually, a rough path etched in the rock.

We attached the ropes to the largest trees across the ledge, and one by one climbed down to the bottom.

Two of the guards led the group, waiting at the bottom to help us down.

A few times the rock came away under my fingertips and I swung away from the mountainside, but I kept my balance and waited with the group for the next climber to descend. We decided to lower Skygge down second to last, and Kara lifted him gently over the edge. As she gradually let the rope go over the cliff, Skygge made his way down slowly.

I sent the rope back up to Kara, and watched nervously as she tied it tightly around her waist. Her white hair caught the sun, shining silver as it swirled around her head in the wind.

She hopped onto the ground, coiled up the rope and tucked it over her shoulder. We stopped at the lake to collect more water, filling cups and bottles. The sun had disappeared behind the trees, and we started a fire to rest for the night. Tomorrow was the final push, if we started early we could make it to the Forge.

Chapter Thirty

Six hours of hiking through the forest, snow falling thick and fast around us and we came to a clearing in the trees.

"I see it!" Isha cried, pushing past us to run through the icy grass. The villagers hurried up the old stone path, making their way back to the Forge's huge iron door.

Kara hung back, watching the rest of the group return to the old wooden building.

Loria stood anxiously next to her, picking at the hem of her sleeves.

"You won't stay just one night?" Loria frowned, and I shook my head.

"If I leave now I can make it home by tomorrow evening." I sighed, and hugged her. "I will visit you soon."

"And you'll tell your people that things are different now? You'll tell them we mean them no harm?" Loria grabbed my shoulders and didn't let go until she was satisfied I would pass on the message.

Kara gave me a long hug, and smiled at me sadly.

"You've taught me a lot Alura." She said, taking my hand. "Be safe, and return soon."

Harker brought out a leather bag, handing it to me awkwardly. "There's plenty of food and water in here, it'll get you home." He told me, and I grinned.

"Thank you." I hugged him, swinging the bag over my shoulder and waving to the children gathered at the Forge's entrance.

...

I take a deep breath.

I knocked nervously on the door, my hands shaking. The door opened slowly, and a small face peeked out suspiciously. I was suddenly conscious of my appearance... would they recognise me like this? I was muddy to the knees, my hair hung damp around my face, and my clothes were dirty and torn.

"Alura?"

I stared at the face examining me on the doorstep, and realised with a shock that it was Lila.

"Lila, it's me." I smiled, a single tear running over my filthy cheek. She screamed, grabbing me and wrapping her arms round me as if I might disappear if she let go.

"Lila!" A rough voice shouted from inside the house, and my father came running outside. When he saw me, he stopped still.

"Maure! Arna!" He croaked, still staring at me as if he didn't believe it was actually me standing in front of him.

Moments later, my mother and sister burst through the doorway, and I sobbed as Maure fell to her knees.

"I thought you were gone." She sobbed, shaking her head. My mother grabbed me, hugging me and kissing my forehead. Lila stood gripping my cloak and I took in the moment as Skygge trotted up to Maure, licking the tears from her cheeks. I pulled away from Lila, my mother stepping back to let me go forward. I reached down and pulled Maure to her feet.

Wrapping my arms around her I smiled. I was home. I was safe.

"You came back." Maure sobbed, her shaking hands holding my own. "Where were you? I thought we would never see your face again."

"I've been far away." I nodded, wiping the tears from my face. "But I'm back, and things are going to change."

Acknowledgements

I'd like to start by thanking my mum. You have taught me so many things over the years, but one lesson really stuck with me and helped me in writing this book: patience is a virtue (not a bird shoe). Thank you for working harder than anyone I know to give me what I have now.

Thank you to my grandparents for being there for me through everything.
You have always made me feel like I can achieve anything I put my heart into, and I would not have been able to write this book without your support and encouragement.

Thank you to Jake for being my best friend and the best brother I could ask for. This book is for you.

Thank you to Phil for putting up with my constant panicking and changes in direction when it comes to writing this book. I could not have finished this mammoth project without your help and support. You are greatly appreciated.

Thank you to my cousins Henry, Honour, Bethany, Hannah and Madeline for inspiring me to write this story. I hope you enjoy it.

Tusen takk, Gaby for reading my book and being my first beta reader! I really appreciate the time you put into helping me write this novel!

And finally, thank you to J. R. R. Tolkien and Rick Riordan for inspiring me to write fantasy.

About the author

Elfie is a fantasy loving English Literature and
Creative Writing student from the UK. When
 she doesn't have
her nose in a book,
she can usually be
found playing with
her two dogs, Lucy
and Honey.
Writing has been Elfie's passion since she was
a child, and her main goal in writing is to
create magical stories that are accessible to
children and adults with dyslexia, as well as
fantasy fans everywhere.

The Forest Of Fallen Stars is her debut children's novel, and the first book in a new trilogy.

The story continues in *The Girl Who Breathed Fire*

Coming soon

Book Club Questions

Which scene stuck with you the most?

What surprised you the most about the book?

Would you read more books by this author?

Did this book remind you of any others?

Which character did you relate to the most?

Which character was your favourite, and why?

Did you feel connected to the setting?

Did you anticipate the ending?

What animal would you want as a companion?

Q&A with the Author

How did you name the characters?

Some names were researched before I started writing the story, but other names came to me more naturally. I always knew Alura and Eslanda's names, but Harker was one I had to research.

When did you start writing The Forest Of Fallen Stars?

I started writing Forest in 2018, and worked on it a lot over the summer of that year. I revised many different versions of the story, and quite a few scenes were cut or changed before the version you have in your hands finally evolved!

How do you get motivated to write?

I usually look to my favourite authors for motivation when it comes to sitting down and drafting a new story. Adrienne Young is an incredible source of inspiration and motivation when it comes to writing, and I admire her immensely.

What's the best thing about writing?

Being able to explore all the new and exciting ideas that are always swimming around in my head. I often get to know my characters so well, that it seems almost impossible not to tell their stories.

If you could travel to any fictional world, where would you go?

I would go to Hobbiton, without a doubt! I'd have second, third and fourth breakfasts, and enjoy the beautiful scenery.

Find Elfie on the Internet...

www.EnchantedElfie.co.uk

@enchantedelfie

Enchanted Elfie on YouTube

Review The Forest Of Fallen Stars on
www.Goodreads.com.

Printed in Great Britain
by Amazon